DATE DUE		
11-28-92 · OCT. 22 1997		
OCT. 23 1992 11/20/98		
NOV. 1 1 1989 12/18/98		
DEC. 1 7 1993 FEB 2 2 2001		
DEC. 3 0 1993		
OCT 1 9 92 JAN 2 6 1999		
OCT. 1 8 1995 APR 0 5 '00		
NOV. 3 1996 APR 0 4 '00		
NOV. 2 2 1995 JUN 0 3 '00		
DEC. 2 2 1995 MAR 2 2 2001		
APR 1 4 2001		
SEP. 1 2 1997		

THE HOUSE
ON
BOSTWICK SQUARE

Also available in Large Print
by Velda Johnston:

Along a Dark Path
The Crystal Cat
Fatal Affair
House Above Hollywood
A Howling in the Woods
The Light in the Swamp
Masquerade in Venice
The Mourning Trees
Shadow Behind the Curtain
Voice in the Night

THE HOUSE
ON
BOSTWICK SQUARE

Velda Johnston

G.K.HALL&CO.
Boston, Massachusetts
1988

JOH
LARGE
PRINT

Published in Large Print by arrangement with
Dodd, Mead & Company, Inc.

G.K. Hall Large Print Book Series.

Set in 18 pt. Plantin.

Library of Congress Cataloging in Publication Data

Johnston, Velda.
  The house on Bostwick square / Velda Johnston.
      p.   cm.—(G.K. Hall large print book series)
  ISBN 0-8161-4377-3
  1. Large type books.   I. Title.
[PS3560.O394H59   1988]
813'.54—dc19   88-16431

For Jeanne Waring

One

THE HANSOM CAB moved off through the early dark, the rattle of its tall wheels loud in the quiet London square. For a few moments, Laura Parrington stood motionless on the sidewalk, one hand holding a valise and the other her daughter's small, slightly moist hand. She looked at the house. So here it was, the place where her beloved had been born and had grown to handsome manhood, only to meet a violent and still unexplained death on the other side of the Atlantic.

The glow from a gas street lamp about ten feet away showed her that the Parrington house looked much like its neighbors here on Bostwick Square. The same handsome facade of rough gray stone. The same white steps leading up to a small, white-pillared porch. The same iron-railed areaway with a stair leading down to what Laura knew was a cavernous kitchen and a servants' dining hall. As in the case of its neighbors, vertical strips of light shone between not-quite-drawn draperies on the ground floor. Yes, the Parrington house looked to be what it was, the well-kept city residence of a successful man. In the case of this particular man, success had brought not only riches but a summons to Windsor Castle, where a queen in perpetual mourning had tapped his shoulder with a sword held in one plump hand, thus transforming him from plain Joseph Parrington to Sir Joseph.

No, there was nothing in the appearance of this house to indicate that it held some dark and secret fury, something that had driven young Richard Parrington from its portals, across the Atlantic, and ultimately, perhaps, to his death in the shadows beneath a Manhattan elevated railway.

BRITISH NOBLEMAN'S SON DIES IN PLUNGE FROM SECOND AVENUE EL, the headline in the New York *Clarion* for October 5, 1888, had read. A subhead added, POLICE UNCERTAIN AS TO WHETHER CAUSE WAS SUICIDE OR MURDER.

Even in her first shock and raw grief, Laura had thought of the smile that the headline would have brought to Richard's lips. "Americans think," he had told her soon after they met, "that any Englishman with a title, even a knighthood, must be an aristocrat. My father started out as a clerk in a shipping line office. *His* father went to sea from the time he was fourteen until the time he died, at the age of thirty-four, in a fall from a ship's mast."

The memory of Richard's smile, Richard's voice, brought her grief so sharp that he might have been dead for only hours instead of almost six months. Grimly she fought back the pain.

She fought back, too, a reluctance to enter this house, which had spat out one of its sons as if he had been something distasteful, and where her own welcome would be at best a tepid one. Suddenly, she wished that she could lead Lily down the dark street until they found a cab, a cab that would take them back to Euston Station, where they could catch a train for Liverpool and its berthed transatlantic ships.

Such thoughts were futile. There was scarcely enough money in the black poplin reticule dangling from her wrist to take them to the railway station and back to Liverpool, let alone across the ocean.

Lily was looking up at her. The blond hair, even lighter than Richard's, fell from beneath the little brown velvet bonnet. Below the blue eyes, the same shade as Richard's, there were dark smudges of fatigue. Laura had awakened the child before daylight in the cramped cabin they shared with two middle-aged spinsters, so that as soon as the ship docked they would be able to go ashore and catch a London train. It had been a long day for a six-year-old.

Fleetingly, Laura wondered if the Parringtons would expect to see Lily in mourning. Well, it couldn't be helped. There had been little money to spend on small black garments. Besides, ever since her father's death, the once-lively child had been too quiet, too well-behaved. Laura had not wanted to weight her small spirit even further with the very symbols of loss.

"Mama, are we here?" A worried note in the soft little voice. Laura wondered if she had communicated to Lily some of her own anxiety about what awaited them beyond that tall door with its heavy-looking brass knocker. She hoped not.

"Yes, darling, this is where your grandparents live."

Tightening her grip on the small hand, Laura led her daughter up the steps.

Two

ONLY A SECOND or two after Laura knocked, the door opened. A woman stood there, silhouetted against the lighted hall. To judge by her dark dress with its neat white collar, she was an upper servant. Laura could not see the woman's expression clearly, yet she caught a distinct impression of embarrassment.

"Good evening. I'm Mrs. Richard Parrington."

The woman's voice held a nervous friendliness. "Please come in, Mrs. Richard. I'm Mrs. Mockton, Sir Joseph and Lady Parrington's housekeeper."

Laura led her daughter across the threshold and set down her valise. The soft light of gas wall sconces illuminated a wide hall paneled in some lustrous dark wood and set with doors, all of them closed. To Laura those rows of closed doors seemed chill and unwelcoming. The wall space between the doors was hung not with the family portraits that a man of less humble origin might have placed there, but with oil landscapes in heavy-looking gilt frames. Dark red carpeting, soft and thick underfoot, covered the hall and also the stairs, rising to a more dimly lit floor above.

Mrs. Mockton said, "And this must be Miss Lily."

Half expecting her daughter to drop the curtsy she had taught her before they left New York, Laura wondered if small girls were supposed to curtsy to housekeepers. But apparently the child was too tired to remember what she had been taught. Her only response was a shy smile.

Mrs. Mockton was in her late fifties, Laura saw now, a somewhat stout woman with graying dark hair and a plain, large-featured but appealing face. A horsehair brooch held her starched white collar in place.

Mrs. Mockton said, "Sir Joseph and Lady Parrington are sorry not to be able to welcome you. They have retired for the night. They instructed me to tell you that they will see you in the morning."

Now Laura understood the woman's embarrassment. The hands of the tall clock standing against the right-hand wall pointed to five minutes of nine. At this early hour the Parringtons had chosen to "retire" rather than greet their son's widow and small daughter.

"Lady Parrington is not strong, you know. And Sir Joseph felt he might be coming down with a cold. Now I'm sure," Mrs. Mockton went on quickly, "that you'll want to go up to your rooms."

She reached down and lifted the valise. Embarrassed to have a woman more than twice her age carrying her luggage, Laura said, "Oh, please—" But already Mrs. Mockton was climbing the stairs. Holding her daughter's hand, Laura followed.

The housekeeper said over her shoulder, "I suppose your trunks will be arriving to-morrow?"

There was only one trunk. "Yes, or so the purser aboard the ship told me."

They had almost reached the landing when a door on the lower floor opened. It closed almost immediately, but not before Laura had caught a glimpse of a tall, dark-haired man.

Sir Joseph? No, the man she had seen looked young. Richard's brother, Justin Parrington? No, Richard had told her that Justin, six years younger than himself, was fair-haired.

And so, she realized with a tightening of her nerves, the tall man must have been

7

Clive Parrington, Richard's older half-brother, Sir Joseph's son by his first wife.

They were on the second floor now. Mrs. Mockton opened a door and then stepped aside for Laura to enter. "This is your room, Mrs. Richard. It overlooks the garden. Miss Lily's room is through that connecting doorway."

The glow of gas wall jets showed Laura a four-poster mahogany bed with a massive highboy to match. Green-flocked paper covered the walls. The rug, old but rich looking, displayed pale pink roses against a dark green background. At the two windows, draperies of heavy green velvet framed cream-colored lace curtains.

It was a handsome room. But with another stab of longing Laura thought of how much more to her taste the larger of the two bedrooms in that Manhattan flat had been, and not just because she had shared it with Richard. Since there had been no money for luxurious draperies with which to shut out the light, plain muslin curtains had hung at the windows, stirring with every breeze. A braided rag rug had left much of the golden oak floor bare. Because the house, once a private mansion, had been converted to flats only the year before, the room's wallpaper—

daisies on a blue background—had been clean and bright.

But this richly handsome room, too, held at least one fresh, simple note. On the small mahogany table beside the bed stood a milkglass vase holding yellow daffodils. Laura suspected that placing them there had been Mrs. Mockton's idea. She said, looking at the flowers, "How pretty!" English springs must come earlier, she thought. Back in New York, daffodils would still be only green shoots above the bare earth.

Mrs. Mockton's smile was gratified. "They're the first of the season," she said. "Now, the w.c. is across the hall. There's a wash basin with running water there, too. Your bathtub is behind that screen over in the corner. The maids will bring up hot water whenever you like."

Laura felt more than a little shocked at the thought of servants toiling up two long flights of stairs with cans of hot water. In some ways, apparently, America had surpassed the mother country. That block of flats near New York's Gramercy Park had sheltered no rich people. Most had been young couples like Richard and herself. And yet each flat had had its own bathtub, with water piped down from a tank on the roof.

"Now, wouldn't you like a little supper?" Mrs. Mockton asked. "I could send up a tray of boiled chicken and some vegetables and a sweet."

As a matter of fact, Laura had been hungry for hours and knew that Lily must have been, too. Aboard ship that morning she had eaten heartily of porridge and bread and sausage and had urged the child to do the same, hoping that the food would last them until they reached London. But the train had been late in its departure from Liverpool and during its journey to London had suffered frequent unexplained delays. Famished, Laura finally had led her daughter to the restaurant car, only to recoil in horror from the prices listed on the menu. Two shillings—almost a half-dollar—for a meal of roast beef, vegetables, and an apple tart! Finally Laura had ordered a meat pie (nine pence) and two plates and, despite the waiter's disapproving look, had divided the pie between her plate and Lily's.

"Supper would be very nice, thank you."

"A girl will be up with a tray in about twenty minutes. And I'll send someone up immediately to help you unpack."

"Oh, please don't." Bone weary, Laura felt it would be easier to unpack her and

Lily's few belongings herself rather than supervise some perhaps talkative maid.

"Very well, madam. Breakfast will be in the dining room from seven-thirty on. If you come down fairly early, you'll see Sir Joseph and perhaps Mr. Clive before they leave for the shipping company offices."

"But not Lady Parrington?"

"No, she has breakfast in her rooms. But I'm sure she'll see you later on in the morning."

No mention of the Parringtons' youngest son, Justin. Perhaps he no longer lived at home. By now he must be twenty-three or -four, old enough to have set up his own establishment.

"Well, good night, Mrs. Richard. Good night, Miss Lily."

Mrs. Mockton went out. As she walked toward the stair landing, she thought, poor little lady! So pretty with all that dark hair and those big brown eyes, but so sad and lost-looking in her black hat and black redingote.

Again she felt a surge of indignation. Why had Sir Joseph and his wife left it to *her* to greet their son's widow? Did they hope that by treating her coldly they could induce her

11

to take herself and their grandchild back across the Atlantic?

Harriet Mockton had been with the Parringtons for more than thirty years, starting out as a kitchen maid when the first Mrs. Parrington had been alive. (And that's what she had been, plain Mrs. Parrington. It wasn't until ten years after her death that Sir Joseph had received his knighthood.) She felt she knew almost everything about the Parringtons. She knew the exact nature of the illness, always referred to delicately as "female complaint," that afflicted Lady Parrington from time to time. She knew that for a while fifteen years ago, the family's shipping line, Parrington Limited, had been in financial straits, a fact Sir Joseph had managed to hide from most of his employees and all of his competitors. She knew the real reason why Mr. Justin had been suspended from Eton for a term. (Imagine the little devil breaking into the liquor cabinet in the headmaster's study and drinking so much brandy that in the morning they had found him asleep on the floor!)

But what she did not know was why Mr. Richard, at only twenty-two, handsome, popular, and the apple of his mother's eye, had gone to America. All she knew was that the

12

cause of his departure must have been something cataclysmic, so much so that Lady Parrington had taken to her bed for several months and Sir Joseph, usually an abstemious man, had sat up drinking alone in the library night after night. As for Sir Joseph's eldest son, Mr. Clive, he had abruptly stopped seeing a Miss Crichton, although everyone had expected the announcement of their engagement.

The reasons for all this the Parringtons had managed to keep from her. Oh, she knew the official explanation, the one circulated by the Parringtons among their social and business acquaintances. But she found it hard to believe that Mr. Richard's gambling debts, however frequent and excessive, had been the sole reason for his exile.

She was also ignorant of why the Parringtons were so reluctant to have Mr. Richard's young widow under their roof. She only knew that, five months after the news of his son's death, a cablegram from America had arrived for Sir Joseph. It had been sent, Mrs. Mockton was sure, by Mrs. Richard. Instantly, the grief-laden atmosphere of the household changed to one of agitation. Sir Joseph had conferred in low tones and for long intervals with his wife behind the closed

13

doors of her sitting room and with his eldest son in the library. Eventually, though, they must have decided to send her a letter, or more likely a cablegram, asking her to London, because Mrs. Mockton had been given orders to prepare two rooms for the widow and her child.

On the ground floor she turned and walked back along the hall toward the servants' stairs, hoping that Bessie had kept her promise to stay awake until after the newcomers' arrival.

Laura carried the valise into her daughter's room. It was smaller than her own room, but to Laura's eyes it was more attractive, with blue wallpaper striped with silver, a pearl gray carpet, and a three-quarters-width bed and chest of drawers of golden oak. She undressed her sleepy child and pulled a nightgown over her head. "Now pop into bed. I'll bring you your supper when it comes."

"Mama, why does that lady call me *Miss* Lily? And why does she call you Mrs. Richard?"

Laura felt too tired to try to explain to her small American daughter the intricacies of the British class system. "It's just a way they have over here. I'll tell you more about it tomorrow."

She moved back and forth between the rooms, hanging the contents of the valise in the massive wardrobe in her room and the smaller one in Lily's. All the time she was thinking of that dark man she had glimpsed briefly as she climbed the stairs. And she was remembering a hot summer night of several years before in that third-floor flat, a night when Richard's hoarse voice, charged with rage and fear, had brought her out of deep sleep. By the dim, refracted glow of a streetlamp she saw that he was sitting up in bed. "Damn you, Clive!" he was saying. "Damn you to hell!"

She too sat up and grasped his shoulder. "Richard! Wake up!"

In reply he lashed out with one arm, catching her across the bridge of her nose. She gave a cry and slumped back onto the pillow.

That woke him. "Laura? Laura, sweetheart! Oh, darling, what did I do?"

He fumbled with matches and lit the small oil lamp on the stand beside the bed. Blond hair rumpled, face appalled in the soft glow, he asked, "Did I hurt you?"

"Not really."

"I was dreaming."

"I know. You dreamed you were having a fight with your brother. Your brother Clive, I mean."

He said after a moment, "I told you we never got along."

"But it was more than that, wasn't it?" She recalled his dreaming voice, hoarse with hatred. Never before had she heard his voice sound like that. She said with an intuitive leap, "It was because of him that you left England, wasn't it?"

"In a way. I guess that without him my parents might have—but that's all water under the bridge. And it was all to the good, too." He smiled down at her. "If I hadn't left England, I wouldn't have met you. You're sure I didn't hurt you?"

"My nose tingled for a moment. It's fine now."

"Then let's go back to sleep, darling. At seven I've got to rise and shine for Mr. Vine." Mr. Vine was the president of the stock brokerage house where Richard was employed.

Now, hanging one of her two black dresses in the closet, she wondered grimly what that dark man downstairs would say if she demanded to know why he had been so determined that his young half-brother be exiled.

Someone knocked. Laura opened the door to a girl with carroty hair, a freckled face, and a warm smile. She carried a large tray laden with covered silver dishes, a teapot, and silver and china for two.

"My name is Bessie, ma'am. I've brought you and the little lady some supper."

Laura opened the door wide. "Come in. I suppose you can put the tray on that bench at the foot of the bed."

When Bessie had deposited her burden, she straightened up and gazed appreciatively at the new arrival's lustrous dark hair and her oval face set with wide-spaced eyes, a slightly aquiline nose, and a soft-looking mouth contradicted by a firm chin. A plain girl herself, Bessie was one of those rare people who can admire without envy qualities they themselves lack.

She was also an inquisitive person, and she felt curious indeed about this American lady. As a devotee of *Housemaids' Own*, a monthly publication, she had read many novelettes about poor girls who married the sons of earls and dukes and such. True, Sir Joseph wasn't an earl, but he was rich. And according to Cook, his daughter-in-law had been poor—an orphan, no less, raised by a preacher and his wife. Not some posh C. of E. reverend, but more like Dwight Moody and the other Americans who came over here sometimes to the Metropolitan Tabernacle and shouted from the pulpit that most Londoners were going to burn in hell. Only, Cook said, the evangelist who raised Sir Joseph's daughter-in-law hadn't been famous like Mr. Moody.

"You must be awfully tired, ma'am."

"Yes, I am," Laura said pointedly. "As soon as my daughter and I have our supper, we're going to sleep."

Still Bessie lingered. "Are you sure you don't need anything more, ma'am?"

"I'm sure."

"After this, shall I bring cocoa at night? A mug for the little girl when she goes to bed, and later on a mug for you? Maybe I could brush your hair for you, too." She imagined how the American lady, soothed by cocoa and the smooth strokes of the brush, might in time confide to her the whole sad, romantic story.

"That would be nice, if it's not too much trouble." Laura lifted the cover from one of the silver dishes. Sliced chicken, still so warm that a little steam rose from it. "This looks delicious. Thank you, Bessie."

At Sir Joseph's order, a fire had been kindled in the library, even though the night was not really cool. He had gone to his bed nearly an hour before, leaving his son alone in the shadowy, book-lined room.

Clive Parrington stood beside the fireplace, his gaze fixed on the still-glowing logs. His face, bathed in the reddish light, was thin and dark with a high-bridged nose. From a few early childhood memories as well as photographs, he knew that his was a masculine version of the face of his mother, the first Mrs. Parrington.

He was thinking of the young woman he had seen climbing the stairs with her small blond daughter. So that was what Richard's widow looked like, a fragile-appearing brunette with a determined-looking chin. For some reason, Clive had expected her to be a rather plump blond. In the one letter Richard had sent from America, or at least the only letter Clive had seen, he had not described his wife but had merely said he was marrying the adopted daughter of some Methodist evangelist.

How much of the truth did Laura

Parrington know? Having been his wife for about seven years, surely she must know some of it.

Damn her. Why hadn't she stayed on her side of the Atlantic? Given the opportunity, the family would have sent her money to stay where she was. But instead she had come here, where her presence at the very best would mean apprehension and strain.

And at the very worst—

He seized the brass-headed poker and savagely prodded the almost-spent logs, sending up a swarm of sparks and a few tongues of flame.

Three

SHE WOULD GO to sleep as soon as she had finished supper, Laura had said. But after she had placed the tray of empty dishes out in the hall, and kissed Lily good night, and stretched out in bed in her darkened room, she found that she could not sleep.

Perhaps it was a sense of the still largely unknown house stretching around her. Perhaps it was the faint scent of hyacinths rising from somewhere below to drift through those elaborately patterned lace curtains. It was a sweet but troubling fragrance, reminding her of florists' stands along Madison Avenue, reminding her of how in the spring Richard would bring home a pot of plump blue hyacinths or jonquils wrapped in a cone of green paper, his face wearing that self-conscious look that a man so often has when he presents flowers to his lady.

Or perhaps it was that, after two weeks on the ocean, her body still had not accustomed itself to dry land. In Liverpool that morning, she'd had a strange feeling that the earth rocked gently beneath her feet, just as the ship's deck had. Now in the wide bed she felt a return of that rocking sensation, as if she were back in her narrow bunk aboard ship or, for that matter, back in her cradle.

Not that she could remember being in her cradle, of course, or anything else of the first two and a half years of her life, not even her parents. It was only through a tintype that she knew what they had looked like. Dark and thin and attractive, their tintyped images had conveyed an impression of youthful liveliness, despite the stiffness of their pose, with Amelia Barret, wearing the voluminous skirts of the eighteen sixties, seated in a chair and Thomas Barret standing beside her, one elbow placed on the photographic studio's version of a broken Greek column, one hand holding his stovepipe hat. Strange to think that two people so vital looking had succumbed, only four years later and within days of each other, to a typhoid epidemic that swept the town of Rochester, New York.

Because the young couple had had no close relatives willing and able to be responsible for the small girl, Laura would have been placed in an orphanage if it had not been for her mother's cousin, Martha Harmon, and her husband Benjamin.

Laura had no memory of the Harmons coming up to Rochester and taking her back to Brooklyn and there legally adopting her, thus changing her name from Barret to Harmon. Her first memory was of sitting in a patch of sunlight on a carpet in that Brooklyn house. She could recall the faint smell of dust and the threadbare pattern of the carpet, pink roses on a tan background. There must have been a wind outside because the window frames were rattling. An old house but far from solid, it had been a farmhouse before the growing city engulfed it. In a rocker nearby Martha Harmon— Aunt Martha to Laura—sat with her smooth gray-brown head bowed, her gaze fixed on the black sock she was darning. In nearly all of Laura's memories of Aunt Martha, the woman's head was bowed.

From beyond the door to his study Laura could hear the Reverend Harmon—Uncle Benjamin to her—rehearsing a sermon in his strong, rather hoarse voice. She could hear the floor creak and knew that he was striding up and down, a thin man, enormously tall to Laura, with bony features and bright dark eyes set under bushy brows. Even though she had not understood most of what he said, the phrase "loose women," whoever they were, had lingered in her memory from that long-ago day of sun and wind.

The Reverend Harmon had denounced all the deadly sins, from gluttony to sloth, but like St. Paul he had thundered loudest against lust, not only to the small congregation in his Brooklyn church but to much larger crowds that he addressed each spring, when he began his evangelical tours of towns in upstate New York and Long Island. And of course he was much concerned about protecting the innocence of the girl child in his charge, so much so that when Laura reached her teens, he decided that, even though funds were as always in short supply, she should transfer from public school with its "rough-talking" boys to Miss Wilfred's Day School for Young Women.

There the Reverend had miscalculated. With boys around to overhear them, Miss Wilfred's pupils might have behaved with more maidenly reserve. But as it was, they gathered in giggling groups before and after school, exchanging bits of information—and misinformation—about what was referred to as the facts of life and reading copies of a newspaper published by the notorious Claflin Sisters, who advocated not only votes for women but free love as well.

Laura was uncomfortably aware at Miss Wilfred's that the girls sometimes giggled about the effect of Reverend Harmon's fervid sermons, especially those he preached when he traveled through the blossoming countryside. On those journeys Benjamin Harmon drove himself and his wife and his adopted daughter in his buggy. His much-patched revival tent followed them on the Long Island railway. In each town volunteers from among local churchgoers helped him erect it on some vacant lot.

Once a senior girl at Miss Wilfred's said to Laura with a sly smile, "Do you know what I overheard my father say about Reverend Harmon? He said that nine months after he

24

holds a revival in town, the birth rate always goes up."

"I don't understand what you mean," Laura answered coldly. But at fourteen, she did understand, more or less. And she knew there was some truth in what the girl had said. Often at revivals, when she sat on the platform with Aunt Martha while the Reverend urged his hearers to resist the lures of the flesh, she had observed young men and women stand listening near the tent's rolled-up walls, only to slip away into the darkness before the "altar call," the exhortation for sinners to come forward and be saved.

She had also become gradually aware during her growing-up years that Uncle Benjamin's sermons had a stimulating effect even on himself. Often on Saturday afternoons, after he had rehearsed the next day's sermon, she would hear him say to his wife, "Martha, I must speak to you." Head bowed, Aunt Martha would follow her husband up the stairs. The door of their room would close and remain that way for half an hour or so.

By the time she was fifteen she knew that Benjamin Harmon had become increasingly conscious of her own ripening femininity. Not that he ever said anything about it or made any gesture beyond an occasional awkward pat on her shoulder. But she was often aware of a constraint in his voice and of his troubled gaze dwelling on her when he thought she wasn't looking.

Laura knew he was a good man, sincere in everything he said and did. But that knowledge did not lessen her uncomfortable awareness of his inward struggle. What was more, he seemed determined that she discourage young men who manifested an interest in her. Each of them, according to Benjamin Harmon, had something wrong with him. The young man who lived two doors away and asked to call on her had parents who were Universalists, "the next thing to atheists." As for the older brother of one of Laura's classmates, he had been seen "hanging around a poolroom." Even young men whose families were members of his own congregation had something wrong with them. They lacked "good sense," for instance, or were "bone lazy."

Once at Sunday dinner, after the Reverend Harmon had forbidden her to go on a Hudson River cruise to which she had been invited, Laura asked, "Is it because boys are invited, too?"

He answered that honestly, even though

she could tell he wished she hadn't asked it. "Yes. You are too young for such parties."

Laura was aware that Martha Harmon, head bent over her plate of roast lamb, had cringed, as she always did at even a hint that someone might dispute her husband's judgment. Nevertheless, Laura said, "Lots of girls are *married* at sixteen." When there was no reply she added, "Don't you want me to marry?"

"Of course, in due time. Your Aunt Martha and I were both twenty-seven when we were married. That seems to me a suitable age."

Twenty-seven! Why, that was middle-aged.

That night, an unusually warm one for April, she sat curled up on the floor beside the window sill in her darkened room, inhaling the fragrance of newly opened narcissus in the backyard below and wondering what was to become of her. She had a chill sense that she might still be sitting there not only at the age of twenty-seven, but at thirty-seven and beyond. And yet what could she do? Defy the kindly couple who had saved her from an orphanage and run away? Run away with whom? Certainly a girl with no money and no means of making a living couldn't run away alone.

On a summer night a little more than two years later, she met Richard Parrington.

It was the first night of a scheduled two-week revival in Hempstead, Long Island. Seated with Aunt Martha and a number of local church dignitaries on the platform, Laura could look out over the crowd who had assembled from all over the island, traveling by buggy and farm wagon and railroad. Light from the big oil lanterns affixed to the tent's ridge pole shone down on their upturned faces.

On one face in particular.

He sat in an aisle chair near the rear of the tent, a man with waving blond hair. Even at that distance Laura could tell that he was handsome indeed and not much older than herself.

A local minister led the congregation in prayer. Then, while a pianist played "Shall We Gather at the River?" on a rented upright, Laura and a thin, sandy-haired youth, the son of a Methodist deacon, walked to the rear of the tent to take up the collection.

As she neared the blond man, she saw his blue eyes widen. She had been right. He was superlatively handsome, with a short, straight nose that gave him a merry look, a well-cut mouth with a full lower lip, and a square chin.

He was also very drunk.

Later on, whenever he said that he had fallen in love with her at first sight, she would answer, "You couldn't have. You were too drunk."

"I wasn't *that* drunk."

But he had drunk enough whiskey that she could smell it. So could others. His nearest neighbors, a middle-aged couple, sat several seats away, their faces rigid with disapproval.

At the rear of the tent Laura took a long-handled collection basket from its wooden rack and then, pulse rapid, started back along the aisle. Not looking at the blond man but very aware of his gaze fastened on her face, she extended the basket to the middle-aged couple. The husband put in a quarter. Laura drew the basket back and held it in front of the blond man. After a moment his gaze dropped from her face to the basket.

"Oh!" he said. "Oh. Quite!"

Three words only, but enough to tell her that he was English. What was a handsome, drunken, and, to judge by his clothes, well-off young Englishman doing at a Benjamin Harmon revival?

He fumbled inside a fawn-colored jacket a shade lighter than his waistcoat and finally brought out a brown leather wallet. Shocked, Laura saw him drop a dollar bill into the basket. She wanted to say, "Take it back! Nobody gives that much." But of course she couldn't say that.

She and the thin youth finished the collection. The blond man remained in his seat through the Reverend Harmon's sermon. "A Latter-Day Sodom," but left before the altar call.

He was back the next night, cold sober, and took a seat in the otherwise empty back row. When Laura held the basket out to him, he said softly, "My name is Richard Parrington." He dropped a dollar bill into the basket. "You're Dr. Harmon's daughter, aren't you?"

So he had managed to find that out. She wanted to say, "Don't call him Doctor. He doesn't have a degree." But feeling flushed and much younger than eighteen, all she could do was murmur, "Adopted daughter." Then she moved quickly away, lest Uncle Benjamin notice that she was lingering with one member of the congregation.

The next night Richard Parrington said softly, even before he reached for his wallet, "I want to see you, alone." He paused. "Where are you staying? In this town, I mean?"

As she lay awake the night before she had decided, with feverish defiance, what she was going to say if he asked that question. "Fifty-eight Emory Street," she said. When in Hempstead the Harmons always stayed at that address, the home of a Baptist minister.

His next words told her that he had also managed to learn that the Reverend Harmon did not welcome gentleman callers. "I've rented a rig. I'll be waiting a few doors away at eleven o'clock tonight." He dropped a bill into the collection basket.

The Baptist minister and his wife locked both the front and rear doors of their house at night. But fortunately the room they always assigned to Laura was on the first floor, opposite the kitchen. As soon as she heard the grandfather clock in the front hall strike eleven, Laura climbed over her window sill into the light of a three-quarter moon. As she moved swiftly and quietly along the drive, she was aware of the fragrance of white roses growing over the front fence.

A buggy stood a few yards away at the

curb. Praying that no one was watching from an upper window, Laura hurried to it. Richard extended a hand and helped her in to the seat beside him. He slapped the reins, and the horse, a roan, drew them down the street and around the corner.

Richard Parrington said rapidly, "You'll want to know things about me. I'm twenty-three years old. I was born and raised in London. My father is Sir Joseph Parrington. He owns a steamship line. For the past year I've lived in a boarding house in Manhattan." He paused. "I'm a remittance man."

"A what?"

"To put it bluntly, my family sends me a certain sum each month in return for my agreement to stay out of England."

She cried, incredulous, "But why?"

"I gambled. It started my first year at Cambridge, and it got worse. I piled up debts. My father finally got tired of paying them, and—well, he threw me out."

Gambling was a grave sin. Still, fathers had forgiven their sons for worse. It seemed to Laura that this Sir Joseph must be a harsh man indeed to have insisted that his son leave not only his home but his country.

She asked, "What do you do here? What sort of work, I mean."

"No sort. There hasn't been any reason to."

She had heard that in the old countries many rich men's sons never sought gainful employment. Still, the idea shocked her American sensibilities to the core.

"But I'll work if you want me to. Several young men at my boarding house sell securities. I think I might be good at that."

"You'll work if *I* want you to? Why, I have nothing to do with it."

"Oh, yes you do. I want to marry you. If you want to keep me waiting for six months, I'll wait. I'll wait one year, two years, but I do intend to marry you."

Heart racing, hands clasped in her lap, Laura remained silent. They had turned onto an unpaved street lined with darkened houses set far back on deep lawns. In the bright moonlight, elms cast moving shadows over the cracked sidewalks.

Finally she said, "Do you still gamble?" knowing that she would still want to marry him no matter what his answer to that was.

"Sometimes." His tone was so somber that she shot him a quick glance. "Sometimes the impulse just—overwhelms me. But I think I could resist if you would marry me."

They were nearing the end of the street.

Beyond lay open fields. Laura could smell moist earth and growing green things.

She said, "Uncle Benjamin would never consent."

"Is that what you call him?"

She nodded.

"Yes, I know how he feels about suitors."

"You know? How?"

"The morning after I met you, I asked the old clerk at the hotel where I'm staying if he knew anything about the evangelist preaching in the tent. He said he always went to hear the Reverend Harmon, and that in fact he'd been there the night before. Then he smiled and said, 'Young fellow like you, I'll bet who you're really interested in is that daughter who always sits up on the platform. You might as well give up before you start, son. The Reverend don't allow any courting.' "

After a moment Richard added, "I'd better take you back."

The buggy turned. For a while as they rode back through the sleeping streets, the clop of the roan's hoofs loud in the stillness, they said nothing. Then Laura asked, "How did it ever happen?"

"How did what happen?"

"Someone like you coming to that revival meeting."

He laughed. "I'd come out here to attend a wedding. A man at my boarding house married a Hempstead girl. There was a lot of champagne at the reception. Afterward I went with several of the men guests to a saloon. I was walking around, trying to clear my head, when I saw that tent and heard singing. I think I had some vague notion that it was a play or a circus or something."

After they turned onto Emory Street, he drove past the Baptist minister's house and stopped the buggy near the spot where he had waited for her. He turned to her and reached out and she went into his arms, feeling as if it were the most natural thing in the world. When their kiss, a long one, ended, he said with his lips close to her ear, "Will you meet me here at the same time tomorrow night?"

"Oh, yes!"

He held her for a moment longer. Then he said, "You'd better go in now."

Four

TWICE MORE THAT week she slipped out of that ground-floor window. Then Richard went back to Manhattan to seek—and find— a job as a securities salesman.

In July, when the Reverend Harmon brought his wife and adopted daughter back to the old Brooklyn house for a brief respite between revivals, Laura crept down the stairs one night, valise in hand, and slipped out the unlocked front door to where Richard waited in a rented carriage. She spent the rest of the night in a room that Richard's sympathetic landlady had prepared for her. In the morning she and Richard were married at City Hall.

Immediately afterward she sent a telegram to Uncle Benjamin and Aunt Martha telling them the news, asking forgiveness, and saying that she and Richard would see them that afternoon.

When they reached the Brooklyn house, only Aunt Martha received them, her eyes red-rimmed. Her husband, she said, would not see them. Instead he was upstairs, praying for the strength to forgive them both.

Laura pictured him beside the big double bed, on his knees but not with head bowed. His face, eyes closed, would be upturned to the ceiling while he addressed his God respectfully but forcefully and on almost equal terms.

"He says he thinks he can find it in his heart to forgive you but not to ever see you again."

"Oh, Mrs. Harmon!" Richard said. "Surely he doesn't mean that."

"Oh, yes he does," Martha Harmon said, and burst into tears.

Laura put her arms around her. "Don't cry, Aunt Martha. You and I will still see each other. You will visit us, won't you?"

"If Benjamin allows me to," she said, between sobs. "Oh, Laura! How could you get married before Benjamin even met your husband?"

Laura said gently, "You know it would have made no difference how often he met someone I wanted to marry. He'd still have been opposed."

Weeping, Aunt Martha didn't answer.

Laura and Richard felt subdued later as they rode in a horse car back across the brand-new Brooklyn Bridge. But they were too much in love to remain depressed for long. For a while they both lived at Richard's boarding house. Then in September they rented a third-floor flat near Gramercy Park and furnished it sparingly. Already Laura was pregnant, and so they were saving to buy a house on the city's outskirts in a few years' time, someplace with a yard where their son or daughter could play.

When her child was born, Laura's disappointment that it was not a boy lasted all of about five minutes. When she saw the round little head with its wisps of pale gold hair and a face that was not red and wrinkled like most newborns' but smooth and fair, she thought, how could I have ever wanted anyone but her?

About an hour later she said to Richard, "I thought of calling her Lily."

"With that hair and complexion, what else could we call her?"

Although their flat was not directly on Gramercy Park, the tenants of their building were allowed to have keys to the fenced area in the center of the square with its trees and benches and gravel walks. On pleasant days Laura would sit there, book in hand, beside Lily's baby carriage until it was almost time to greet Richard when he came home from his job with an investment firm.

He was doing well as a securities salesman. Even though they saved money, they
could still afford at least once a week to leave
Lily in the care of a middle-aged couple on
the first floor and go out to dinner or a play.
On Sundays, with Richard pushing the carriage, they window-shopped the big new department stores on Union Square. After Lily
learned to walk, they took her to the zoo on
Sunday or on steamboat rides up the Hudson.

Sunny as their life was, there were dark
intervals.

The first had come when Laura was eight
months pregnant. Richard did not come
home to dinner that night. Instead a messen-
ger boy arrived with a note that said, "I
must have dinner with a customer, darling.
Don't wait up for me."

She didn't wait up, but she did wait, lying
alone in the dark while a clock in a nearby
church steeple struck ten, eleven, midnight.

A little after one she heard his key in the
lock. She sat up, fumbled with matches, and
lit the bedside lamp just as he appeared in
the doorway. He looked awful in the upward-
striking light, his face white with shadows
under the blue eyes. He might have been
close to forty rather than in his early twenties.

"Richard! What is it? Are you hurt?"

"No."

"Sick, then? Have you been drinking?"

"No." He sat down on the edge of the bed and began to take off his coat.

"Then what is it?" When he didn't answer, she asked, "Have you been gambling?"

"Yes." His pale face turned toward her.

Angry that he had broken his promise to her but relieved that nothing worse had happened, she asked, "Did you lose a lot?"

"No. As a matter of fact, I won." He gave a rigid smile that held no humor at all. "I've grown rather adept at your American game of poker."

He didn't look as if he had won. He looked as if he had lost, lost more than just money. She had a sense of something dark hovering over him, something that had been there all the time although she had not glimpsed it until now.

She said, "Next time you might lose."

"There isn't going to be a next time!"

The harshness of his face and voice forbade any sort of answer. Then he said, more quietly, "Turn out the lamp, Laura. Let's go to sleep."

A week later, dusting the top of his bureau, she saw his savings bank passbook lying there. Usually he carried it with him. Because he worked on Wall Street, near both their savings and commercial banks, it was natural for him to handle all their financial transactions. He gave Laura enough cash at the beginning of each week to cover food and small personal expenses. Larger purchases she charged to an account he had opened for her at a Union Square department store; he paid the bills by check. Usually she paid no attention to such matters, just assuming that their nest egg was growing slowly but steadily. Now, though, she opened the passbook.

At some time on the day he had not come home for dinner, he had withdrawn a hundred dollars from their savings. For that poker game, wherever it had been? Almost certainly. But he said he had won. If so, he had not deposited his winnings into their savings account. He hadn't even replaced the hundred dollars.

It must be like a sickness, she thought miserably, the sort of sickness of the spirit that impels some other men to get drunk every once in a while and stay drunk for days and days. Did he feel it was a kind of sickness? She recalled his saying, that first night they drove through the Long Island moonlight, "Sometimes the impulse just over-whelms me."

Did he want to discuss it with her as a form of sickness? Had he left that passbook here with its damning evidence as a kind of silent cry for help? Remembering the harsh-ness with which he had ended their conver-sation when he finally came home that night, she could not believe that he wanted to talk about it on any terms. Nor did she want to. After all, he had said it would not happen again.

But it did. Not often; two or three times a year. Laura became able to discern what she thought of as a "spell" coming on. For a few evenings he would seem both silent and rest-less, hiding his face behind an outspread newspaper for fifteen minutes or so, then getting up to go to the window and stare down into the street. Then would come the night when she would lie alone in bed, wait-ing for the sound of his feet on the stairs.

He was always contrite afterward. And each time he would say that no great finan-cial damage had been done. He had lost only a little, or broken even, or actually won.

He did not again leave his savings pass-book lying around, nor did she ask to see it. If he were losing money, she did not want to quarrel with him about it. Such clashes might spoil the long, happy intervals between those lonely evenings, intervals when they found joy in each other and their child. Again and again Laura told herself how much more fortunate she was than other wives she had heard of. In her case, there was nothing to complain of except a solitary evening now and then.

When Lily was five, the Reverend Benjamin Harmon died. As Laura and Richard stood with a score of others at the graveside in a Brooklyn cemetery, she felt sorrow not only for his death but for the fact that he had never become reconciled to her marriage and had never even seen Lily.

Two weeks after that, Aunt Martha, unable to bear living alone, had gone to Kansas to live with her sister and her sister's farmer husband.

On a fall night about a month later, Richard not only failed to come home for dinner, he did not come home at all.

At six-thirty in the morning, too distraught even to feel the fatigue of a sleepless night, she got up and dressed herself and her drowsily protesting daughter. Her hands were icy with the conviction that something had happened to Richard. Perhaps the police at the precinct house a few blocks away could help her find him.

She led Lily down the stairs and left her with the Bensons, the kindly couple in the first-floor flat. Then she went out into the chill morning light. A uniformed policeman and a man in a gray suit were coming down the sidewalk. They reached the foot of the steps just as she did.

Her agitation must have shown in her face, because the gray-suited man said tentatively, "Mrs. Parrington? Mrs. Richard Parrington?"

"Yes!" She clutched his arm. "What has—"

"I'm Sergeant Wales, of the thirteenth precinct, and this is—"

"Something's happened to my husband! Hasn't it, hasn't it?"

"Mrs. Parrington, we'd better go inside."

She remembered climbing ahead of them up the familiar stairs, only now they seemed unreal, like a flight of steps in a bad dream. When they were inside the flat, the gray-suited man suggested that she sit down, and she sank into a chair. There was a roaring in her ears. Through it she caught bits of what he was saying. "Near Eighteenth Street, under the El," and, "wallet and watch missing," and, "about three last night."

Don't faint, she ordered herself. Fainting was a luxury she could not afford. She had to plan how to shield Lily from the full force of this blow.

When the plainclothesman told her that she must "come down and identify your husband," she managed to get to her feet unassisted.

Now, lying in bed in this luxurious house an ocean away from that flat, she thought, "And I got the two of us over here. At least I managed that."

The day's accumulated fatigue suddenly overwhelmed her, and she slept.

Five

THE BED GAVE slightly under someone's weight. Laura opened her eyes to morning sunlight. In her white flannel nightgown, Lily knelt on the bed, gazing at her mother from between twin falls of pale yellow hair. Laura swept back the bedclothes, and the child snuggled down beside her.

"Any bad dreams?" Since her father's death, Lily had often awakened whimpering or even screaming in the night. As nearly as Laura could make out from the child's half-incoherent accounts, all the dreams had concerned helplessness in the face of danger. Lily had found herself all alone on a dark street, with "a giant" coming toward her. Or she was alone in the flat with the lights out and "some kind of animals" outside in the hall, throwing themselves at the door to break it down.

"No, Mama, I didn't have any dreams."

Laura's arm tightened around the fragile shoulders. She took that as a good sign, a sign that she had been right to swallow her pride finally and ask the Parringtons for shelter. Despite its unfamiliarity, the very solidity of this rich man's house and its far remove from the four rooms where she had first been told of her loss apparently had made the child feel safer.

A light tap at the door. "Come in," Laura called.

Bearing a white wicker tray, Bessie came into the room. This morning a ruffled cap hid most of her carroty hair. She beamed at the two in the big four-poster. "Good morning, ma'am. Good morning, miss." She touched a spring under the tray, and its legs descended. Settling the tray across Laura's lap, she said, "Here's your morning tea. Shall I bring up some milk for the young lady?"

"Oh, no, thank you. Lily can have a sip of my tea." She looked at the clock on the fireplace mantel, a white china one with a pair of gilt cupids leaning against its rounded sides. The hands pointed to eight. "Besides, we'll be going down to breakfast soon."

Bessie looked disconcerted. "Both of you, ma'am? Why, we thought Miss Lily would have her meals in the old nursery upstairs."

Laura recalled then something Richard had told her. Among the English upper classes, children do not take meals with grownups.

"If it's all right with you, ma'am, I'll be giving her her meals. Mrs. Mockton said that Lady Parrington said that temporary-like I'll be excused from my other duties"— she pronounced it *jooties*—"and be Miss Lily's nanny."

A nanny. Of course. In the homes of the rich, children were cared for by servants. And in this case some sort of nursemaid would be necessary, since Laura intended to find gainful employment as soon as possible.

She looked at Lily. Thank heaven the child seemed to have taken to Bessie. She was regarding the freckled face under the ruffled cap with shy friendliness. "That arrangement will be fine," Laura said, "except that I'd like her to go on sleeping in the room next to mine." Never in Lily's short life had more than one wall separated her from the parental bed. Laura did not want her exiled to another floor of this big house.

"Just as you say, ma'am. Let me pour your tea."

As the pale liquid streamed from a silver pot into a cup of thin pink china, Laura again glanced at the clock. "I had expected to be called earlier," she said. "I wanted to see Sir Joseph. Mrs. Mockton said he breakfasts at seven-thirty."

"She thought it better to let you have your sleep out, ma'am, you looked that tired last night. But you'll still probably see Sir Joseph at breakfast. He told James—James is Sir Joseph's man—that he wanted to sleep late because of his cold." She stepped back from the bed. "Shall I come back in twenty minutes?"

"Twenty minutes?"

"To take Miss Lily up to the nursery."

"Oh, yes, thank you."

Less than half an hour later, she climbed with her daughter and Bessie up to the next floor. Here the light brown hall runner was economically thin, and the walls were covered with white plaster rather than paneling. Laura guessed that the closed doors on either side led to servants' bedrooms.

The nursery, a big corner room, was shabby but cheerful. Light poured through thinly curtained windows onto a worn floral rug with a low table and three straight chairs—two child-size, one for an adult—set in its center. Two battered desks with slanted hinged tops stood against one wall. Near them, above a bookcase holding a few books, hung two framed prints of knights in armor.

On a table against the opposite wall, near an old cupboard, stood a rectangular gas plate. A small pot of porridge bubbled on one of its rings. Noticing the direction of Laura's gaze, Bessie said, "Sir Joseph had that put in two years ago, so that when the servants are sick they can still have warm food. Things get pretty cold by the time you carry them up three flights."

Then this man she was about to meet could not be entirely hard of heart, despite his banishment of his son for a regrettable but not uncommon weakness. At least, when modern invention made it possible for him to do so, he'd tried to make his servants' lives a little more comfortable.

Her gaze moved to the two small desks.

"This must have been the nursery when my husband was a little boy."

"Yes, ma'am. And before him this was Mr. Clive's nursery, and after him Mr. Justin's, although all that was long before my time. I came here only three years ago."

Well after Richard had gone to America. But Bessie knew that he had been the family black sheep, paid to stay on the other side of the ocean. The knowledge was plain in her curious and yet sympathetic eyes.

Numb with fatigue the night before, Laura had not felt a full awareness that Richard had spent the first twenty-two years of his life in this house. But now she could almost see him when he had been his daughter's age, seated at one of those desks over there, chubby fingers gripping a crayon, his fair head bent over a sheet of drawing paper.

Trying to ignore a stab of pain, she said, "Now you be a good girl, Lily." She smiled at Bessie and then left, descending from the shabby but bright servants' floor to the more thickly curtained corridor below and then to the still darker one below that. How strange of the rich, she thought, to live behind thick draperies of satin and velvet, leaving sunlight and air to flood only the children's school and play areas and the rooms, empty by day, where servants slept.

She had no trouble finding the dining room. Its door stood open. Halting at the threshold, Laura looked at the man who arose from a chair at the end of the long oval table. He was a stocky man, bald except for a fringe of white hair. His plain, large-featured face and his broad hands, with their fingertips resting on the highly polished table, might have belonged to a day laborer. But his gray eyes were alert and shrewd, the eyes of a man capable of rising from humble origins to wealth and power. He looked nothing at all like Richard.

He said, "You must be Laura. Come in, my dear. I'm Joseph Parrington."

His accent, too, was not at all like Richard's. That must be, she realized, because he had been born in Bristol and had not, like his sons, attended Eton and Cambridge.

She walked into the room. "Best not to come too close," he said. He gave her a forced-looking smile. "I seem to have taken cold."

"Yes, the housekeeper told me. I'm sorry, Sir Joseph."

He did not look even slightly ill. Could it

be, she wondered, feeling chilled, that he didn't even want to touch her hand? Was she *that* unwelcome? Perhaps. But it seemed to her that if she could glimpse anything at all behind that forced smile, it was some kind of fear rather than repugnance. But why? What threat could his widowed daughter-in-law and his small granddaughter bring to this house?

He said, "Help yourself to some breakfast, my dear."

As she turned to the long buffet table, she realized that despite her anxiety she was hungry. She placed scrambled eggs and two broiled kidneys on a floral-patterned plate and took a piece of toast from the rack. Sir Joseph pulled out a chair for her several feet from his own and then went back to his place at the head of the table.

Seated, Laura found herself facing a full-length portrait of a blond woman that hung above the white marble fireplace mantel across the room. The severe black riding costume she wore only emphasized the frail-boned femininity of her figure and of her lovely face with its wide-set blue eyes. Laura felt no doubt that the blond woman was Richard's mother, Sir Joseph's second wife.

A strained silence lengthened. Laura ate

several forkfuls of scrambled eggs, and her father-in-law sat with elbows propped on the table and hands linked above his own plate with its remnants of toast and bacon strips. Finally he said, "Your communication was of course a terrible shock to us."

Murmuring something appropriate, she wondered which "communication" he meant, her letter telling of Richard's death or the cable five months later announcing her intention of bringing Lily to her grandparents' home.

"I am sorry indeed," Sir Joseph said, "that you were left in such straitened circumstances."

It hadn't been until more than a week after Richard's death that she had realized how straitened her circumstances really were. The money in her and Richard's joint checking account had been enough to pay for the funeral, that pitifully brief funeral, in a "mortuary chapel" with only herself and Lily and a few men from Richard's office and the Bensons from downstairs in attendance. As for food expenses, Richard had given her a week's housekeeping money the day before his body was found. In a gray fog of grief she made trips to the grocery store, cooked meals.

Then one morning she found she had less than five dollars in her purse. Well, no matter. There was that twenty-thousand-dollar life insurance policy Richard had taken out several months ago, despite her protests that the premiums would cost too much, that he was young and healthy, and that she didn't even want to *think* of such matters. Twenty thousand would keep her and Lily a long, long time. Lethargic with sorrow, she had not done anything about that policy yet, but tomorrow she would go down to the insurance company offices a few doors from the securities firm where Richard had worked. At the same time she would present his savings account passbook to the bank and find out how she could withdraw from it, even though the book had been issued in his name only.

But first she would have to find the book. It had not been on his body, even though his checkbook had been. Surely that passbook was somewhere in the flat.

She found it, finally, under the paper lining the shelf in his closet.

Because of those nights two and three times a year when he had come home late, she had expected to find their savings smaller than they might otherwise have been. But she had not expected to find a balance of less than seven dollars.

With fingers that felt like wood she leafed through the little book, scanning the record of more than six years. That first withdrawal of a hundred dollars. Then, a few months later, a similar withdrawal. Then three, spaced months apart, of a hundred and fifty. The next one had been for two hundred, and the next two for two hundred and fifty each.

And so it had gone. He had deposited money, usually each week, but never enough to make up for those withdrawals of ever-increasing amounts. The last one, made the day before his body was found, had been for six hundred dollars.

Passbook in her hand, she stared at the wall. For the first time it occurred to her that something other than his gambling might be involved. She had a sense of some hidden implacable enemy, someone who might have bled Richard dry and then, one way or another, brought about his death.

But she found it impossible to imagine the nature of such an enemy. No, Richard had gambled the money away, plunging more deeply as time went on in an effort to make up his losses.

Much as she needed that almost-seven dollars, she did not take the passbook with her when she went down to Wall Street the next day. She could not bear the thought of the look—sly? pitying? avidly curious?—that she might see in the eyes of the teller who had paid out those cash sums to her husband.

In the insurance company office, Laura asked for a Mr. Clemshaw, the agent who had sold Richard the policy. After an interval she was shown into his cubbyhole office. He rose from behind his desk, a thin young man with rimless spectacles. Unaccountably, he looked embarrassed. "Sit down, please, Mrs. Parrington."

Sitting in the straight chair opposite him, she said, "I'm sure you know why I've come." She laid the policy on his desk.

He said, not touching it, "I don't know how to tell you this except straight out. Our company has already decided to disallow this claim."

"Disallow?"

"We've decided not to pay it, Mrs. Parrington."

She said, too dumbfounded to feel anything at all for a moment, "Not pay it! Why, you have to pay it!"

"No, Mrs. Parrington. Where there is strong evidence of suicide, the law does not require insurance companies to honor claims. As I'm sure you recall, the coroner attributed your husband's fall from that elevated track to 'causes unknown.' "

Laura had been aware of it, but numb with grief, she had given it little thought. To her it seemed obvious. Richard's wallet was gone. His watch had been torn from its chain. Perhaps the robber had struck him over the head, leaving him dazed. Anyway, he had staggered out onto the track, plunged to his death—

She cried, "He couldn't have killed himself! He was happy. He had a good marriage, a child, a promising position—"

"Mrs. Parrington, I hate to ask you to do anything so painful, but please look at the facts. If someone had already robbed your husband, what reason would he have had for forcing him to walk out onto the tracks for several yards and then pushing him to the street below? Furthermore, if for some strange reason the thief had pushed him, your husband in all probability would have fallen backward. Instead he fell face downward to the street.

"No, Mrs. Parrington, we feel sure that your husband disposed of his wallet and watch somewhere—perhaps dropped them from the bridge into the river—in the hope that the coroner's verdict would be murder, or at least robbery followed by accidental death. Then he climbed up to the el station, walked out along the tracks, and jumped.

"Now you are free to sue the insurance company, of course, but you would be wasting your money. I liked your husband, Mrs. Parrington, but even if I hadn't liked him, I wouldn't give you bad advice. Please believe me."

After a moment he added, "Surely you must have some other assets."

She said, with an effort, "Yes." There was the engagement ring, set with a small diamond, that Richard had insisted upon giving her, even though she hadn't been able to wear it until after they were married. There were the gold-and-ruby cuff links and shirt studs that went with Richard's evening clothes, garments he'd had no reason to wear at any time during their marriage. There was his pair of sterling silver military brushes and his silver-backed tortoiseshell comb. Surely all those articles would bring several hundred.

Still, even though she had no skills except those of a housewife, she would have to find work.

Rising, she placed the policy back in her reticule. "Good-bye, Mr. Clemshaw."

Now, in the Parrington dining room, the silence stretched out, broken only by the subdued clink of Laura's fork against her plate. Sir Joseph was not even pretending to eat. At last he said, "I should have thought my son would have taken at least some measures to protect his wife and child in the event of his death."

"Oh, but he did!"

She told him about the insurance policy and Mr. Clemshaw. She wanted to add, "Do *you* think Richard killed himself?" But that was something you could not ask of a father, not even one as estranged from his son as Sir Joseph had been.

He said in a perfectly neutral voice, "I see." He was silent for a moment and then added, "I trust you have been made comfortable here." Again she sensed in him a mixture of embarrassment and fear. The embarrassment she could understand. The Parringtons had tried to ignore their daughter-in-law and their grandchild both before and after their son's death. It was the fear she could not fathom.

She said, "We're both very comfortable, thank you."

"Good." He pulled a thick gold watch from his waistcoat pocket. "Please excuse me. I must go to my office now." He stood up and then added, "In case no one has told you, luncheon is at one. I won't be here. My son and I go to the club. But I'll see you tonight at dinner."

She inclined her head, "Good-bye, Sir Joseph."

About a minute after he left the dining room, she heard a carriage start up outside and drive away. She wondered how long the Parrington coachman had been waiting at the curb for his employer.

Six

FOR A WHILE she sat there looking down at her empty plate. She felt not only puzzled but profoundly disappointed. All the way across the Atlantic she had kept hoping that her reception would be at least a little cordial.

Well, surely Lady Parrington, if only as another woman, let alone as Richard's mother, would be more sympathetic. And then there was Lily. Neither of the Parringtons had seen their grandchild yet.

Sir Joseph hadn't asked a single question about her. Still, Laura was counting a lot on Lily. Once they did see their granddaughter, Laura was convinced, neither of them would be able to resist that shy smile and those blue eyes and fair hair she had inherited from her father and from the beautiful woman whose portrait hung above the fireplace in this room.

A green baize door opened, and a uniformed maid, a thin, middle-aged one Laura had not seen before, came in with a tray in her hand. "Good morning, ma'am. My name is Martha."

Laura smiled. "Good morning."

"Shall I clear away, ma'am, or do you want something more?"

"No, thank you. I've finished."

Before Laura could rise, Mrs. Mockton appeared in the hall doorway. "Good morning, Mrs. Richard. If it is convenient, Lady Parrington would like to see you in her rooms."

Laura rose eagerly. Out in the hall she said, "Lady Parrington will want to see her granddaughter. I'll go up to the nursery and—"

"Begging your pardon, ma'am." Again that embarrassment on the broad face. "Lady

Parrington doesn't feel up to seeing Miss Lily yet. Her nerves have been really bad these past few days."

Disappointed and with faint but growing anger, Laura wondered how any woman's nerves could be that fragile, so much so that she could not receive any well-behaved six-year-old child, let alone her own grandchild. But then, in all fairness, Lady Parrington had no way of knowing Lily was well-behaved. Perhaps she visualized a child who might race around the room, insist upon handling valuable ornaments, and throw a temper tantrum if thwarted.

Well, with all of them living under one roof, it couldn't be more than a day or two longer before the Parringtons saw their grandchild.

"I'll take you up to Lady Parrington," Mrs. Mockton said. She turned toward the staircase and then stopped short.

A young woman Laura judged to be about her own age, a fashionable figure in a close-fitting gray dress with a bustle and a gray toque with a half-veil, was descending the stair. At its foot she said, "Good morning, Mrs. Mockton." Then, turning to Laura, "You must be Laura Parrington. My name is Valerie Lockwood, and I'm a distant family connection." She laughed. "Very distant. I'm Lady Parrington's second cousin, once removed."

"How do you do?"

Valerie Lockwood had glossy chestnut-brown hair and a face that was both pretty and pleasant. Her gray eyes held neither embarrassment nor unease but only a friendly welcome. Perhaps it was just the strain of her first few hours in this house, but Laura felt an impulse toward grateful tears.

"This morning I had breakfast with Cousin Dorothy. Lady Parrington, I mean. She told me she hadn't seen you yet."

"I'm going up to her rooms now."

"Don't let me keep you. I have shopping to do. Anyway, I'm sure we'll see a lot of each other. My father and I live only two doors away, so I'm always popping in and out." Her smile widened. "Good-bye, Laura. Is it all right for me to call you that, since in a way we are related?"

"Of course."

"And please call me Valerie. Good-bye, Mrs. Mockton." She again smiled at Laura and then turned toward the front door, where the middle-aged maid who had cleared the breakfast table waited to let the visitor out.

When the door had closed behind her, Laura said, "Such a nice person."

The housekeeper nodded. "Yes, we're all fond of Miss Lockwood. As she said, she comes here often. I think the poor young lady finds her own house a bit too quiet. Her mother died two years ago, and her father can't seem to get over it. He's turned in on himself, so to speak."

Laura followed the housekeeper up the stairs and along the corridor, past her own room to one three doors down and on the opposite side of the hall. Mrs. Mockton knocked. After a moment the door opened.

A tall woman of about thirty-five, with dark hair braided in a coronet around her head, stood on the threshold. In her brown alpaca dress she looked not fat, merely big-boned. Her face was plain, with a large nose and a too-heavy jaw. By contrast, her gray eyes were quite beautiful.

Their expression, though, was a shock, especially after Valerie Lockwood's friendliness. This woman did not look merely uneasy or embarrassed. For the first time under this roof Laura saw real animosity in another person's face.

For a few seconds Laura was too bewildered even to feel resentment. What had she

64

done, or was supposed to have done, that a complete stranger should regard her with such hostility?

The woman said, before the housekeeper could make the introduction, "I'm Cornelia Slate, Lady Parrington's companion. Come in, please." Her nod to the housekeeper was one of dismissal.

Cornelia stepped back and, when Laura was over the threshold, closed the door. Laura found herself in a sitting room that reminded her of the inside of a jewel box. Elaborately looped pink satin draperies at the window framed curtains of thick Brussels lace. On the floor was an oval Aubusson rug, also predominantly pink. A dressing table was set with crystal perfume and lotion bottles. And there were numerous small tables holding gold-framed photographs and miniatures, and Dresden shepherdesses, and miniature Wedgewood trays of various shapes.

"In here," Cornelia Slate said. "Lady Parrington is staying in bed today."

Laura followed the tall woman into the adjoining room. Lady Parrington sat propped against pillows beneath the flowered chintz canopy of the big bed, a white marabou jacket around her shoulders. She appeared to be only a few years older than the lovely young woman of the portrait downstairs. It was only when Laura moved hesitantly closer to the bed that she saw that the blond hair had silver threads, and the skin around the eyes very fine wrinkles, like those of an expensive white kid glove.

"My dear," she said, and extended a slender hand that felt almost boneless when Laura took it. Her gaze appeared less embarrassed than her husband's had—perhaps women were better at covering up such an emotion—but embarrassment was there, all right, and in the blue depths of her eyes there was something that at least resembled fear.

"Sit down," she said. "Here, close to me."

Laura sat down in a straight chair with a petit-point seatcover. Cornelia Slate said, "Shall I go now?"

"Oh, no!" Lady Parrington added, to Laura, "For the past ten years Cornelia has been the same as one of the family. Her mother was one of my dearest friends."

But not one of her richest friends, Laura decided. Surely young women who had inherited money did not choose to become companions, not even to someone as gentle-seeming as Dorothy Parrington.

"Then I'll go on with my work." Cornelia Slate walked over to a small armchair in a corner of the room, sat down, and from a basket on the floor beside the chair took up a rectangular frame holding a square of heavy linen, perhaps destined to be another petit-point seatcover.

Laura looked expectantly into her mother-in-law's beautiful although slightly faded face. Surely her first question would be about her granddaughter.

Dorothy Parrington asked, "Did you have a good crossing?"

"Yes. It was quite smooth."

"And your room is comfortable?"

"Oh, yes, thank you." She added pointedly, "We are both very comfortable."

The older woman's gaze seemed to flinch. For a moment she remained silent, apparently at a loss for words, which struck Laura as strange in a woman of her mother-in-law's background. Then Lady Parrington said, "I'm sorry I didn't feel up to seeing Lily today."

"I was sorry, too. I suppose I'm prejudiced, but I think you'll find her a very nice child."

"Oh, yes!" The reply was emphatic. "I'm sure I will."

Laura had been throwing glances around her. The walls in this room were paneled, she saw, an effective background for portraits of men and women in Napoleonic era knee breeches and Empire gowns, and others in eighteenth-century powdered wigs, the men in satin coats and breeches and shoes with high heels, the women in elaborately panniered dresses. There was even one dim painting of a man in an Elizabethan ruff. These were portraits, Laura realized, of her mother-in-law's ancestors, the sort of ancestors that her husband did not have.

Richard had told her that his beautiful mother had not only been descended from generations of landed gentry. Her father had been quite rich, too. Why should such a young woman have married a widower more than a dozen years older than herself, a man who, however successful, was still "in trade"? Sir Joseph was obviously an able man and on the whole Laura liked him, but she found it hard to imagine him, at any time of his life, inspiring headlong passion in a young and beautiful woman. And yet, according to Richard, she had married Joseph Parrington with full parental consent when she was twenty and he was thirty-four, with a three-year-old motherless son to raise.

Laura said, "Thank you for arranging to have Bessie take care of Lily. It isn't really necessary now, but it will be later on."

"Later on?"

"When I find a position."

"A—a what?"

"A position. In America we often call it a job. I'm rather good with a needle. I thought, if you knew of some dressmaking establishment—"

From the corner of her eye she saw that Cornelia Slate sat with her own needle suspended in the air.

Lady Parrington said, "You expect to leave this house each morning and go to some—some—"

"And go to my situation, yes!" She felt her temper getting out of hand and paused until she was in control of it. "I don't want to go on being dependent upon anyone for my support and Lily's," she said. "And yet unless I have some safe place for my little girl to stay in the daytime, I can't earn a living. I found that out in New York. In fact, that is why I came here. You see, I'd thought at first that the answer was some sort of domestic work—"

"Domestic?" Dorothy Parrington's voice was faint.

"Yes. You see, I had no money, only some jewelry and a sterling silver comb and brush set that had belonged to Richard. I managed to sell them for almost five hundred dollars—as much as I'd expected to get—but still, I knew it wouldn't last forever, so I went to this employment agency on Madison Avenue and asked for a post as housekeeper. The woman who ran the agency said that I—wouldn't do."

The woman's exact words had been, "From the viewpoint of an employer, you have two great handicaps. First, you have a child. It's a rare family who would willingly hire a housekeeper with a child. Second, you're young and attractive. The woman you ask to hire you might have a susceptible husband or an almost grown son. You would represent a risk.

"Now let me give you some advice." Despite the hard lines in her face, the eyes behind her steel-rimmed spectacles were kind. "You say you are a good needlewoman. There are several millinery factories down near the Battery. The work is not as hard as in some of the other needle trades. And if you really are good at that sort of work, you should be making a fair amount of wages in time."

Laura cried, "But who will take care of my little girl?" At that moment Lily had been with the Bensons in their first-floor flat. But Laura couldn't expect her neighbors to care for her child day in and day out.

"There are day nurseries for the children of working women. I'm sure that the foreman at whatever company employs you will be able to give you the addresses of some."

Three days later Laura had stood at an ironing board against one wall of a loft, smoothing a length of wide purple ribbon with a heavy iron. The long room was filled with row upon row of women. Seated at long benches, they fitted to wooden head molds the hat "bodies," the horsehair foundations for millinery creations of velvet or satin or felt. Her nostrils were filled with the not unpleasant odor of the sizing with which the horsehair had been stiffened.

Nothing about the job was too unpleasant, although now, at past three in the afternoon, her feet and legs felt tired. True, many of the women were rough talkers, using expressions that she had never expected to hear on a woman's lips. Some of their comments she didn't even understand, knowing only by the ribald tone that they must be indecent. Well, no matter. Words could not hurt her. And at least it was good that they could talk. During the twenty-minute lunch period, while she ate the ham sandwich and apple she had brought to work with her, one of the women told her that in some of the coat-and-dress lofts the women weren't allowed to talk at all, lest it slow their work.

As a beginner, she had been assigned to the simplest and lowest paid job in the place, but the foreman had assured her that if she "worked out well," she would be promoted. Best of all, she had found a safe place where, for fifteen cents a day, she could leave Lily.

The day nursery was in an old frame house on Delancey Street, the only private house remaining on a block of red brick tenements. Its small parlor had been neat and clean. The proprietor, a blonde of forty-odd named Mrs. Cushing, seemed pleasant. She was caring for only a half-dozen children, she said. She provided a good hot lunch, and there was a nice backyard for the children to play in. When Laura had left Lily there that morning, the child had clung mutely to her hand for a moment. Then, with the docility that had characterized her since her father's death, she had allowed the blond woman to lead her away toward the rear of the house.

At quitting time Laura hurried two blocks

through the February dusk to the frame house. For several minutes she waited on the doorstep with growing uneasiness for an answer to her repeated knocks. At last the door opened, and Mrs. Cushing said, "Oh, do come in, Mrs. Parrington." Her smile did not conceal her nervousness. As Laura stepped into the little parlor, the woman added, "Please sit down. I'll bring Lily in a few minutes."

"A few minutes! Why should it take—"

Then she heard it, the distant wailing of her child.

She dashed across the room and, despite Mrs. Cushing's protests, jerked open a door in the opposite wall. She ran down a long corridor and into a kitchen. Its walls were lined with infants in high chairs. She caught an impression that some were crying and that many were runny-nosed. Children of two or three squabbled on the floor's cracked linoleum or toddled across it. The air was full of the smell of boiled cabbage and untended babies.

Laura ran out the back door. At least a dozen more children were here in a high-fenced yard strewn with tin cans, part of a rusting perambulator, and a carriage seat with split seams. Over beside the high wooden

gate a tall girl of about ten with brown pig-
tails was trying to hold on to the twisting,
wailing Lily.

Both children caught sight of Laura. The
pigtailed girl's hands dropped to her sides.
Lily, her wails stilled, ran across the hard-
packed earth and tried to encircle her mother's legs with her arms. The older girl said,
"I was trying to keep her from pounding the
gate and hurting her hand again."

"Her hand! Lily, let me see." Laura looked
at the streak of blood on one side of the
small hand. "How—"

"She got a splinter in it, ma'am. I pulled
it out."

"Oh, Mama!" The upturned face was
streaming tears. "I was trying to get out and
find you. They told me you wouldn't come
back. They told me lots of mothers never
come—"

"Oh darling! Who told you that?"

"Not me, ma'am," the other girl said
quickly. "I'll bet it was Kenny or Billy."

"Well, never mind who it was. Come,
darling. We'll go home."

She led Lily back into the house, through
the noise and smells of the kitchen, and
down the long hall to the parlor. Mrs.
Cushing still stood there, silent and sullen

now. Laura said nothing at all to her. She was afraid that if she gave vent to her anger she would start screaming, and Lily had been through enough that day without witnessing her mother's out-of-control rage.

On the way to the horsecar stop two blocks away, Lily said, "Oh, Mama! You won't leave me there tomorrow, will you?"

Laura's hand tightened around her daughter's. "No, darling."

"Those babies in the kitchen were dirty, Mama. And she gave us cabbage and water for lunch. Oh, Mama! I don't want to *ever* eat cabbage!"

"You won't have to."

That night after Laura had washed the dishes, she sat rocking in a chair with her drowsy daughter in her lap. Never again, she vowed grimly. Never again would she risk subjecting her sensitive, fatherless child to such an experience.

The next day, leaving Lily with the Bensons, she went not to the millinery loft but down to a steamship company office on Front Street. Yes, a clerk told her, she and her daughter could book third-class passage for England on a ship leaving in ten days. From the steamship company she went to the transatlantic cable office and paid what

75

seemed to her a staggering number of precious dollars to send a cablegram to Sir Joseph Parrington, Bostwick Square, London. Her message read: YOUR GRANDDAUGHTER AND I DESTITUTE. ARRIVING LIVERPOOL ON S.S. WILLIAMSBURG MARCH 25. As she put the receipt in her purse, a sustaining anger burned out the humiliation she otherwise would have felt over throwing herself upon the mercies of the Parringtons, who obviously wanted nothing to do with her. They were rich, and Lily was their grandchild. They owed her protection and sustenance. And they owed it also to Lily's mother, at least until she was able to earn a living for herself and her daughter.

Five days passed with nothing but silence from London. Laura pressed grimly forward, refurbishing her clothes and Lily's for the journey, notifying her landlord that they were leaving, selling the apartment's sparse furnishings to a secondhand dealer who agreed not to take possession until after she had left.

Finally a cable, signed Joseph Parrington, arrived. Laura knew that it must have been the product of Lord knew how many hours of agitated family conference. But it consisted of only two chilly words: VERY WELL.

Laura had not been surprised, when the ship reached Liverpool, that no one had been waiting on the dock to greet them.

Now, in her mother-in-law's luxurious bedroom, Laura said, "Don't you know of some dressmaking establishment that would employ me?"

"My dear girl, it's utterly out of the question! If it became known that Richard's wife—" Her voice faltered over her son's name. She began again. "If people knew that Richard's wife had become—gainfully employed—it would cause any amount of talk."

"Then what do you expect me to do?" Laura cried. "Live out my life here on your bounty?"

Something flickered in Lady Parrington's lovely eyes. With sudden certainty, Laura knew that the Parringtons did *not* expect to sustain her for the rest of her life, or even for very long. Rather, they felt sure that in this unwelcoming household she would soon feel uncomfortable enough that she would take herself back across the Atlantic, perhaps with a check for a few thousand pounds in her pocket, and never bother them again.

For a moment she felt bitter enough to say, "All right! Bribe me to leave." But her pride rebelled at the thought. Besides, she reminded herself, neither of her grandparents had seen Lily yet. Surely, once they did, everything would change. They would not want to be separated from their only grandchild by the Atlantic.

Lady Parrington said in a lighter tone, "You've been in this house only a few hours. Must we decide such momentous matters right away?"

"No, of course not."

A silence stretched out. Then Laura said, "Perhaps I had better see if my trunk has arrived."

Lady Parrington leaned forward and covered Laura's hand with her own. "My dear—" Her face was suddenly very pale.

"Yes?"

"About—Richard. Do you think he suffered for—very long? Physically, I mean?"

Seeing the agony in the older woman's face, Laura knew that whatever else might be puzzling and obscure in this house, one thing was plain. Dorothy Parrington had loved the son who had resembled her so much, loved him with the near-idolatry some women feel for their sons.

Laura said gently, "No. The coroner told me that Richard could not have lived for more than a minute or two after falling from that height." She paused and then said, "You loved him very much, didn't you?"

The older woman leaned back against the pillow. "More than I've loved anyone or anything on earth."

Laura stood up. "I'll say good-bye now."

Lady Parrington's face had regained some of its color. "Good-bye. If I'm not up and around tomorrow, perhaps you'll find the time to come in and visit me again."

Find the time! If Dorothy Parrington had her way, it looked as if Laura would have nothing but time as long as she remained beneath this roof.

"Of course." She turned and looked at the woman who sat silent, needlework in her hands. "Good-bye, Miss Slate."

The woman coldly inclined her head with its coronet of dark braids.

Seven

WHEN LAURA REACHED her room, she found that her trunk had arrived. It was a battered but sturdy tin one with a rounded top, perforated in a pattern of circles and stars, that she had bought in a secondhand store on New York's Third Avenue. It looked out of place indeed amidst all that mahogany and Brussels lace and thick carpeting. She closed her door, hoping that she could get the trunk unpacked before some servant came to do it for her.

As she moved back and forth between her wardrobe and Lily's, she was aware of spring sunlight filtering through the lace curtains. Now and then she paused to look down from Lily's window into Bostwick Square. It reminded her of Gramercy Park. It held a similar rectangle of trees and grass and flowers, shielded against invasion by a fence of tall iron pickets. Surely the Parrington household had a key to that gate. After lunch, she decided, she would take Lily down to the little park for an hour or so.

When she went down for lunch, she expected to find the dining room empty. But Cornelia Slate was there, standing beside the buffet and spooning something from a silver covered dish. She gave Laura a cool nod and then carried her plate to the table. Laura picked up a plate, served herself a generous helping of some sort of chicken and mushroom mixture from the silver dish, and then sat down opposite the other woman.

After about a minute, feeling she must

break the awkward silence, Laura asked, "Are you a native Londoner, Miss Slate?"

"Yes."

"Do you have family here?"

"No."

Both syllables had been equally cold. Already hurt and offended by the Parringtons' attitude toward her, Laura found this woman's hostility too much to bear. She gave way to an impulse to bring matters into the open. "Miss Slate, why do you dislike me?"

She had thought that the other woman, challenged, might retreat into a flustered denial of the charge. Instead she asked, after a moment's silence, "What did Richard tell you about me?"

"Tell me! Why, nothing. I can't recall his ever mentioning you."

Cornelia flushed. "That can't be the case. He must have told you at least something about me."

"Must have? Why?"

"Because he and I were practically engaged."

Amazed, Laura for a moment was unable to hide her incredulity. Eight years before, when Richard left England, he had been twenty-two. Cornelia Slate must have been around thirty. And even then, no doubt, she had been plain.

"You mean he asked you to marry him?" With no desire to be unkind, Laura tried to make the question sound not derisive or even skeptical but merely interested.

"Not in so many words." Evidently in response to Laura's tone, Cornelia's was less hostile now. "But he made it obvious that he was very—fond of me."

Laura knew then what must have happened. One of the many nice things about Richard had been his attitude toward women whom other men might have treated with indifference or even scorn. For instance, there had been the young woman who ran a flower stand on the corner of Twenty-Third Street and Madison Avenue. A birthmark covered the left side of her face. Whenever Laura and Richard had stopped there to buy a bunch of flowers, as they often had on their Sunday walks, Richard would manage to compliment the girl on something she was wearing or on the new way she had arranged her quite pretty auburn hair. Once he said to Laura in explanation of his behavior, "You can tell she loves beauty. Probably that's why she became a flower seller. She must need to feel that she's beautiful, too, in at least some ways."

That must have been how Richard, generous in his youth and good looks, had treated his mother's companion. Compliments paid to her fine gray eyes, say. A kiss on the cheek beneath the Christmas mistletoe. Perhaps a few flirtatious remarks. And Cornelia, unlike the flower girl, had taken it all seriously.

"Then there was all that trouble between him and his father over his gambling debts," Cornelia was saying, "and so Richard went to America. But if he hadn't met you, I know he would have come home sooner or later, and his father would have forgiven him, and—" Her voice trailed away.

"But I didn't know you had any sort of prior claim," Laura said gently, "and so you really can't blame me."

Too late, she saw that she had taken the wrong tack. Cornelia Slate did not want her grudge to be met with gentle reasonableness, which to her could appear only as condescension. What she really had wanted was to hear Laura say, "Yes! I knew he was in love with someone back in England, but I wanted him to fall in love with *me*, and after a while he did."

Gray eyes colder than ever, Cornelia pushed her plate away from her. She stood up. "Please excuse me," she said, and walked out of the room.

Telling herself not to be upset, Laura went on eating. She knew that she and Cornelia were unlikely ever to be friends. But in time, surely, the woman's animosity would abate, or at least become less open. She helped herself to a dessert of stewed pears. A few minutes later she left the room.

Across the wide hall a door stood open. Laura could see shelves of books reaching from the floor almost to the ceiling. She walked to the doorway. A girl in a shapeless gray dress and a white frilled cap knelt at the fireplace grate, sweeping ashes with a long-handled brush into a dustpan. The face she turned to Laura, cheerful and ash-smudged, was fourteen years old at most.

"Good afternoon, mum," she said. She did not add her name. Whimsically, Laura reflected that perhaps servants who were extremely young and of low enough status to be assigned to grate cleaning were not authorized to volunteer their names.

"Good afternoon," she said, and stood for a moment looking around the room. All four walls were lined with books. No wonder that, on Sundays too inclement for walking, Richard had liked to read aloud to her, not only from Dickens and Jane Austen, some of whose novels had been part of the curriculum at her girls' school, but from Byron and Gibbons and Melville, authors she had not encountered at the Academy, let alone in the Reverend Harmon's household, where the library had consisted of the Bible, *Pilgrim's Progress*, and Fox's *Book of Martyrs*.

She also saw now that although the Parringtons, unlike some rich New Yorkers, had not as yet installed electric lights, they did have a private telephone. It stood on a table in one corner of the room, a tall, impressive black instrument trimmed with brass.

She turned and climbed the stairs. She reached the landing in time to see two men in blue denim aprons—perhaps the coachman and Sir Joseph's man, James?—carrying her battered empty trunk toward the rear staircase. She climbed another flight and opened the nursery door.

Lily shoved her small chair back from the low table and ran across the room. Just as on that late afternoon in the day nursery's ugly backyard, she threw her arms around her mother's legs. But now her face was not distorted with tears. Instead, she looked more animated than at any time since her father's death.

"Mama, come see what I drew!"

"In just a moment, dear." She looked at Bessie's smiling face. "Has she been a good girl?"

"Mama! Come *see*."

Wryly, Laura reflected that her child was indeed recovering. She had even begun to misbehave a little.

"I said in a moment."

"She's been a very good girl, ma'am," Bessie said.

Laura allowed Lily to lead her over to the table. On a square of drawing paper a green crayon ship with orange smoke coming from its stack sailed over a blue sea. Laura said, "Why, that's the ship that brought us here. That's very good, Lily." She turned to the maid. "I'd like to take her down to the park in the square later this afternoon. Do you know where the key to the gate is?"

"Mrs. Mockton has several. I'll go down and get one for you. But if you're taking Miss Lily to the park, ma'am—"

Turning, she opened the door of the old cupboard and brought out a rolling hoop almost as tall as Lily herself. Attached to it by a string was the flat stick with which to propel it.

"Maybe she'd like to play with this. I understand that all three of the young gentlemen did when they were small."

The young gentlemen. Clive Parrington and later on his half-brothers, Richard and Justin. She grasped the hoop, wondering, if, a quarter of a century ago, Richard's five-year-old hand had touched the same spot.

"Thank you, Bessie."

Eight

IN MIDAFTERNOON SHE sat on a wooden bench in the little private park, warmed by the spring sunlight and warmed even more by the sight of Lily, her small face absorbed as she guided the tall hoop along the graveled walk. For the first time in months, Laura felt a measure of calm and even something like contentment.

True, the Parringtons were a puzzle. But at least now she had some evidence that they were not heartless monsters. Soon, surely, she would learn the cause of their behavior toward her. As for Lady Parrington's horror at the thought of Laura's going to work, she felt that in time she and her mother-in-law could find an arrangement whereby, in some dignified fashion, she could earn a little money, at least enough that she and Lily would not be penniless dependents.

Unless, of course, the Parringtons persisted in their unspoken but obvious intention to make her so uncomfortable that she would leave. But Laura was still confident that they would not persist once they came to know their grandchild. In the meantime Lily, unaware that her grandparents were trying to ignore her, was responding to the friendliness of Mrs. Mockton and Bessie. Perhaps, too, after all those months when she must have sensed Laura's desperate money worries, she was responding to something in the atmosphere of the Parrington house, a sense of a world of solid physical comfort and unassailable financial security, a world where no mother would have to leave her little girl in a place of bad smells and cabbage-and-water meals.

Hands clasped loosely in her lap, she looked around her, pleased by everything she saw. The beds of tulips and fat white hyacinths. The willow trees, turning from early spring yellow to late spring jade, trailing their branches along the path. The well-dressed men and women who now and then moved along the sidewalk outside the fence, and the highly polished carriages whirling through the square, and the row of fine houses across the street. She was even pleased by a patroling constable, tall and helmeted and ginger-moustached, who gave her a respectful salute as he walked along outside the fence. Plainly to him her presence in the private park was proof of superior status. She thought of what his reaction might be if he learned that, only weeks earlier, she had felt grateful for the chance to stand ironing hat ribbons for twelve cents an hour.

From the corner of her eye she saw a tall man climbing the steps of the Parrington house. Clive Parrington? Almost certainly. The shipping line offices, Richard had told her, were just off Piccadilly Circus, less than a mile from Bostwick Square. Evidently, Sir Joseph's son chose to walk there and back. But why had he come home in the middle of the afternoon?

She felt a sudden chill conviction that his intention was to talk to her privately, apart from either of his parents.

Again she thought of the time when, in the throes of a nightmare, Richard had lashed out with his fist and cried, "Damn you, Clive!"

The tall man, taking a key from his pocket, had gone into the house. Her pleasant mood of a moment before shattered, Laura waited. Lily, she observed, had leaned her hoop against another bench and now sat on the grass, gathering dandelions.

Still watching from the corner of her eye, Laura saw Clive Parrington come out of the house and cross the cobblestoned street. He took from his pocket a duplicate of the three-inch-long iron key now in her reticule and opened the gate in the fence. He closed it, its clanging sound loud in the quiet. As he approached, feet crunching over the path's gravel, she turned her face toward him, ready for battle. He halted beside her.

Richard had told her that the first Mrs. Parrington had come from Land's End in Cornwall, a region where, three hundred years earlier, many sailors from the Spanish Armada had been shipwrecked. The result, Richard had said, was that more olive-complexioned people could be found there than in other parts of England.

Laura could well believe that the man beside her had descended from one of those ill-fated Spaniards. True, he was as tall and rawboned as any American frontiersman of Anglo-Saxon descent. His long head and square jaw, too, were typically English. But there was a hint of Latin blood in the dark, slightly curling hair and the dark eyes set under prominent brow ridges.

Fleetingly she reflected how fortunate it was for Sir Joseph's sons that they tended to resemble their mothers rather than him.

He said, almost harshly, "I'm Clive Parrington."

"I know." Her chin lifted slightly. "I'm Laura Parrington, your sister-in-law."

She had expected at least a few polite preliminaries, such as inquiries as to the smoothness of her journey and the soundness of her sleep the night before. Instead he attacked immediately. "Why have you come here?"

"I think my cablegram made that clear." She looked past him. Thank heaven that Lily, still seated on the grass, seemed absorbed in the dandelion chain she was making. "My daughter and I were destitute."

"If you had written to ask for money, we would have sent it."

"Would you have?" Her bitterness flared. "None of you even answered my letter about Richard's death."

The dark gaze did not flinch. "Nevertheless, if you had given us the choice, we would have sent you money."

The choice of supporting her in New York or enduring her presence here.

She said in a low, shaken voice, "I had a *right* to bring Lily here. She is a Parrington. I didn't want you to send me your money, your—your charity. No, it would have been even worse than that. You would have been *bribing* me to stay away, just as you bribed Richard."

Besides, she wanted to add, I hoped that because of Lily you would accept me as part of the family. I was so alone. Aside from any financial considerations, I needed to be part of a family.

But her pride rebelled at the thought of saying anything like that to this grim-faced man, this man who, Richard had felt, had prevailed upon Sir Joseph and Lady Parrington to exile the elder of her two sons.

"Why?" she asked in a low, shaking voice. "Why?"

One of his heavy dark brows lifted. "Why?"

"Why was Richard turned out of his own home."

For the first time she became aware that his face was not only hostile. There was scorn in his expression, too. "Surely you know. After all, you were married to him for how long? Six years? Seven?"

"Yes, I knew that he gambled! And he himself was ashamed of it. It was as if he—couldn't help himself. I realize that it must have been very hard on your mother and father. But was that reason enough to turn your backs on him utterly, not even writing to him in all the years after he left for America?"

Just the faintest puzzlement in the dark gaze. But the scorn was still there. "I hear you want to find some sort of employment."

So he must have seen Lady Parrington during his few minutes in the house. She said, puzzled by his seeming change of subject, "Yes, I don't want to be an idle person."

"Then may I suggest that you apply to some theatrical company? I think you have the makings of an excellent actress. In case no one told you, dinner is at seven-thirty."

Turning, he walked to the tall gate. He unlocked it, relocked it, and then crossed the street to the house.

Laura still sat there, angrier than she had ever been in her life before. So he hadn't found it sufficient to emphasize that she was unwelcome. He had made it clear also that he thought her honest bewilderment over the Parringtons' behavior was all a pretense, a lie, "acting."

Finally she thought, I want to stay here if only to spite him.

Nine

ONLY THE TWO men and Laura had dinner in the dining room that night, Sir Joseph at the head of the long table and his son and Laura facing each other across the lustrous mahogany. Lady Parrington, apparently, was dining with her companion in her rooms.

The atmosphere was as uncomfortable as Laura had expected it to be. While Martha, the middle-aged maid, served a mock turtle soup, Sir Joseph led a strained conversation about the weather. Laura's contribution was the remark that even though London was north of New York, spring came earlier here, to which Sir Joseph replied that it was the warm waters of the Gulf Stream that moderated the English climate. As soon as Martha left the room the talk ceased, only to start up again, still with the weather as the topic, when she came in to remove the soup plates.

It wasn't until Sir Joseph was carving the

saddle of lamb that he said to his son, "Did you see the article on the Besant woman in *The Times* this morning?" Then, to Laura: "I don't suppose you have heard of her."

"If you mean Annie Besant, I have." Annie Besant, freethinker and advocate of women's suffrage. "She's famous in America, too."

"The woman's an agitator, and she ought to be locked up! Surely people in America must feel that way also."

Laura's nerves were tightening. "I suppose some do."

"And what is your opinion of her?" Clive Parrington asked.

Unwilling to back away from the challenge in his dark eyes, she said, "I think that in many ways she is right. Women need to be treated—more fairly."

"Fairly!" Sir Joseph said. "My dear Laura, what are you talking about? What do men strive for if not to make the world as pleasant as possible for their womenfolk?"

Laura thought, Is that what they strive for? Or is it that they feel a human need to exercise their abilities and have the privilege of doing so? Aloud, she said, "Yes, I realize that women of the prosperous classes lead very easy lives indeed. But they're so—helpless."

"Helpless!"

"Yes. If by any chance they are left without economic support, there seem to be only two respectable courses open to them. They can become governesses,—and what a cruel life that must be, learning to love children only to lose them when the children grow older. Or they can become companions, which I suppose can be a tolerable life or an intolerable one, depending upon what sort of employer you have." She thought of Cornelia Slate, no doubt treated well enough, yet so emotionally starved that she had tried to nurture herself with daydreams about having won the love of her employer's son. How much better for Cornelia if she could have become a doctor or lawyer or merchant.

Sir Joseph said, "And what is your solution?"

She said after a moment, "All women should have better educations, or at least a chance at them."

"My dear girl, too much education spoils the bloom on a woman."

Yes, just as too much rain spoils a vintage, and too much exercise makes beef stringy, and too much salt ruins the bread. But women aren't *things*, she wanted to cry out, things to be consumed by the other half of the human race.

She said nothing, though, until Clive again challenged her. He said, with something enigmatic in his dark eyes, "And what do you think about working-class women?"

"Working-class women who are left alone? It's infinitely worse for them." She thought of the women in that millinery loft, many of whom had no choice except to leave their children in establishments like Mrs. Cushing's on Delancey Street. "Some men get richer and richer, paying starvation wages to the women in their employ—"

"Come, come now," Sir Joseph said. "No one starves in England or Europe or America, not in the nineteenth century. There are all sorts of soup kitchens and similar establishments for the really destitute." He colored slightly, perhaps having remembered that *destitute* was a word she had used in her cablegram. "Anyway," he added, "there's no reason to turn society upside down, the way that Besant woman wants to." His gaze shifted to his son. "According to *The Times*, she and some other firebrands are organizing a labor rally in Piccadilly Circus. Let's hope they don't break windows the way they did during that demonstration last February."

"At least not Parrington Limited windows," his son answered.

Silence settled down until Martha came in to clear away the dinner plates. Clive mentioned then that he intended to go to his club after dinner, and his father answered that he himself intended to retire early. As soon as she had finished her portion of the dessert, a concoction of wine-soaked sponge cake and whipped cream that Sir Joseph called a trifle, she asked to be excused and left the room.

Up in the nursery she found that Lily, her supper finished, had started on another drawing, this time of the train that had brought them from Liverpool to London. "Bedtime," Laura said. The child's face fell and then brightened as her mother added, "Once you're in bed, I'll read to you."

Bessie said, "If you like, mum, I'll come down and put her to bed."

"No, thank you." She felt a twinge of something like jealousy. No matter what the rules were among the upper-class English, she had no intention of surrendering her child's care entirely to servants. She crouched beside the battered bookcase. "Is it all right if I take one of these down to our rooms?"

"Why, of course, ma'am."

Laura looked at the titles: *Tales of the Crusades. A Child's History of England. A Page to Sir Galahad.* Oh, here was a familiar title, *Alice's Adventures in Wonderland,* a favorite of both Lily and herself. She opened the book to its flyleaf. With a tightening of her throat she read the words in the graceful, back-slanted hand: "To Richard Forbes Parrington from his mother on his seventh birthday, May 15, 1866."

She said, getting to her feet, "I'll take this one. Come, Lily. Good night, Bessie."

'Oh, not yet, ma'am. I'll bring some cocoa for Miss Lily to drink while you read to her. And later on I'll bring you some for yourself."

"Oh, Bessie! Don't do that. You must be tired."

"Oh, no, ma'am. Caring for Miss Lily is like—like being on holiday compared to my regular work. Besides, I'd like to bring you some cocoa."

Not knowing that to Bessie she was a heroine of romance, Laura felt baffled. "Very well," she said. "Thank you, Bessie."

On the floor below, Laura undressed Lily, put her to bed, and let her finish the mug of cocoa Bessie brought. Then for almost half an hour Laura read aloud about the anxiety-laden White Rabbit and the bad-mannered Dormouse and the bloodthirsty White Queen. As Laura had realized long ago, Alice really wasn't a suitable book for supposedly tender-minded children, yet they loved it. Laura herself, who had not encountered the work until she was almost grown up, still loved it. Her worries momentarily forgotten, and absorbed in the account of the croquet game, she did not realize until she looked at Lily to share her pleasure that the child had gone to sleep, her lashes lying like pale fans on her pink and white cheeks. Laura extinguished the gas jet and went into her own room.

She was partially undressed, seated at the dressing table in petticoat and camisole, her hairbrush in her hand, when someone tapped on the door. "It's Bessie, ma'am."

The girl came in, carrying a brown lusterware mug on a small tray. "I'll put it right here on the dressing table, shall I, ma'am?" She stepped back and looked admiringly at Laura's hair, now released from its Grecian knot and cascading to her waist.

"Let me brush it for you, ma'am."

"All right. Thank you."

For a while Laura sipped her cocoa, and Bessie wielded the brush, the whispery sound of the bristles over the silky hair distinct in the silent room. Then Bessie said, "Can I ask you something."

Laura replied cautiously, "Ask me what?"

"Did you and Mr. Richard meet—romantic like?"

Laura thought of Richard sitting whiskey-soaked in the much-patched big tent, with an out-of-tune piano playing "Shall We Gather at the River?" and moths fluttering around the lanterns hung overhead.

"Well, no," Laura said. In the mirror she saw disappointment in the freckled face. "You see, we met in church."

Bessie brightened. The heroine of *A Pair of Dark Eyes* had met Don Carlos in church. Well, not exactly met him. She had been a housemaid in the castle of his father the Duke for almost a year, although he had never taken any notice of her. Then one day he had seen her kneeling in church, her "lily-white" face, framed in an old lace shawl her mistress had discarded, looking "like an angel's."

True, that was a Catholic church, its being in Spain and all, and the church where Mr. and Mrs. Richard met might have been more like chapel. But still—

101

"Did he fall in love with you at first sight, ma'am?"

"He always said he had."

With a satisfied sigh, Bessie let her hand holding the brush fall. "I lost count, ma'am, but I'm sure it was almost a hundred strokes."

"I'm sure it was, too. Thank you, Bessie."

When the maid had gone, Laura sat looking at her reflection. After the long day during which she had encountered varying degrees of hostility from members of the Parrington household, she both looked and felt tired. But despite the warm cocoa, she felt keyed up, too, so much so that she feared she might lie awake again. If she had some sleep-inducing book from the library below, a history of the East India Company, for instance, or a treatise on the Arian Heresy—

Would it be all right just to slip on a dressing gown? No, she decided. Even though Clive Parrington had gone to his club and Sir Joseph to bed, it still would be indiscreet to risk anyone seeing her out in the corridors in a dressing gown and with her hair streaming down her back. She went to the wardrobe, took down the black dress she had hung there about an hour before, slid it over her head, and did up all the little self-covered buttons from her waist to her chin. No need to take much pains with her hair. She bundled it up into a loose knot and thrust a few tortoiseshell pins in to hold it. Then she slipped out of her room.

Ten

GAS JETS, TURNED low, burned in both that hall and the one on the ground floor. The library door stood partially open. By the glow from the hall she found the library gas jet just inside the door and the brass match container affixed to the wall beside it.

Light bloomed in the silent, book-lined room. Feeling awed, she ran her fingers over the spines of leatherbound volumes. Here in gilt letters were names of authors she had heard of but had never read. Joseph Addison and Aeschylus and Thomas Aquinas. Francis Bacon and Balzac and George Berkeley. Had anyone in this household read all those books? Had anyone in the whole world read so many books? Maybe they were like the porcelain cups some people put in glass china closets, not for use for for show.

She had just taken down *Utilitarianism* by

John Stuart Mill—*that* sounded as if it would put her to sleep—when she heard a key turn in the front-door lock. Her pulse gave a nervous leap. Clive Parrington? It had to be.

But it wasn't. The man who appeared in the doorway was shorter than Clive, about five feet ten inches, and had reddish-gold hair. His eyes were blue. Realizing who he must be, Laura knew that his age was about twenty-four, although his slightly snub nose made him look younger than that, and his reddish-gold moustache—perhaps grown for that purpose—made him look older.

He said in a slurred voice, "Well! Who have we here?" and she realized with dismay that he had been drinking, just as his elder brother had been when she met him for the first time.

He said, walking toward her, "You're Laura, aren't you? Knew you were coming." He seemed pleased with himself for having acquired the knowledge. "Know who I am?"

She replaced the book on its shelf. "I think so. You're Justin. But I didn't know you lived here."

"Don't. Flat of my own in Kensington. Money of my own, too, Grandmother."

Laura gathered that he meant that his grandmother had left him money. Surely it was his maternal grandmother. His father's mother, the widow of a merchant seaman, couldn't have left much of anything to anyone.

"But I still have my room here. Going to use it tonight. They painted my digs today. Smells awful."

He leaned toward her so precipitously that for a moment she feared he was about to topple over upon her. "Pretty woman," he said. "Damned pretty. Sorry. Shouldn't have said *damned*. Pretty, though. Guess that was one way Richard was lucky. Unlucky at cards and all that. I never knew Richard well. Six years difference, you know. I was still at Eton when the family threw him out."

Laura had been about to say good night, slip past him, and hurry up the stairs. But if Justin was in a mood to talk of Richard's exile from his family and his country, she wanted to hear him. She felt no compunction about hoping to extract information from a drunken man. As Richard's widow and the mother of his child, she had every right to know all about him.

But Justin's next words were, "Can you tell me the real reason they did it, threw him out, I mean?"

She said, sharply disappointed, "I should

have thought that you would know all about it."

He shook his head. "No. Away at school, you know. And the Governor and Clive and Mother—what is it you Yanks, say?—played everything close to the waistcoat."

"I think they say vest."

"Anyway, they just kept saying it was his gambling debts. Seemed damned odd that Mother would have let him be thrown out for *that*. Should think she'd have done anything to keep his debts paid if the governor wouldn't. Sold her jewelry. Sold me into slavery. Anything."

"Oh, no, really—"

"Never cared too much for me." He sounded fairly cheerful about it. "Mother, I mean. And I know the governor has felt both his younger sons were a bad show. Shouldn't mind too much. He's got Clive. Wonderful chap, Clive. Could take over the shipping line tomorrow and run it. Never drinks too much. The governor and Mother depend upon his advice. Clive has a really cool head. If I didn't know about the little woman he sees regularly over in St. John's Wood—he doesn't know I know that—I'd say big brother wasn't even human."

Again Justin leaned perilously close.

"Know something? I don't like Clive. He's too bloody serious. Sorry. Shouldn't say that before a lady. Saying *bloody* is much worse than saying *damned*. Mean it, though. Looks down on me because I don't do anything. Why should I? Difference between Clive and me is that my mother is gentry and his mother wasn't. Farmer's daughter. Cornwall."

Before she knew his intention, he kissed her full on the mouth. She stepped back and, too startled to speak, turned toward the door. He caught her arm. "Come, now! Nothing wrong with a brotherly kiss, is there? Brotherly-in-law kiss, should say."

She tried to pull her arm free. "Let go of me," she said softly, fiercely. To her dismay, she felt her loosely pinned hair start to come down.

He caught her other arm. "Don't play the prude. I know you're not. Couldn't be. Married to Richard for years and years. And Richard must have been a real wrong one, one way or another. And you must have known all about it. Stands to reason."

"Let go!" She felt fear, not of him—he was too drunk to be a real danger—but of a noisy disturbance. One of the servants might appear in the doorway, or even Sir Joseph, and see her with her hair down in the embrace of the younger son of the house. Her position here, already anomalous in the extreme, would become completely untenable. The Parringtons would have every excuse to tell her to leave.

"Look even prettier with your hair down," Justin said. He jerked her close to him and covered her lips with his in a long, smothering kiss. She twisted in his grasp, wanting to kick his shin but afraid that he would cry out, awake the household—

Then, hearing footsteps, she realized the worst had already happened. She wrenched her mouth free and looked to her right, expecting to see Sir Joseph's outraged face. Instead she saw Clive Parrington. Fleetingly, she realized that, unable to wrestle free of Justin's embrace, she had failed to hear his half-brother's key in the lock.

He strode across the room, grasped Justin's shoulder, and spun him so that he staggered back against the bookshelves. "What the devil do you think you're doing?"

Justin's eyes looked less bleary than they had only minutes ago. He said sullenly, "It was just a kiss. My sister-in-law, you know. Not that it's any of your bloody business."

"Oh, yes, it is."

"You mean you've already made a claim?"

Clive said softly, dangerously, "I'll overlook that because you're drunk. Now if you came here with the intention of sleeping in your old room tonight, go upstairs. Otherwise, leave the house."

Justin's gaze, angry and almost sober now, went from Clive to Laura and back again. Then he shrugged and walked out of the room. They heard his footsteps on the stairs.

Clive said, "Sorry about this." Then, when she didn't answer, "But what were you doing down here, anyway?"

"Selecting a book! Isn't that what people usually do in libraries? How was I to know that he would come in here, drunk, insolent—"

"Perhaps if you hadn't had your hair down—"

"It wasn't down until after he grabbed me." She seized a handful of hair, started to bundle it to the back of her head, and looked wildly around over the carpet. Not seeing any hairpins, she let her hair fall again.

"How dare you imply it was my fault, even partly? It's what he seemed to be saying, too," she went on, almost incoherently. "Something about how Richard must have been a wrong one, and I must be also, since

I was married to him all those years. It was the same way you were talking in the park this afternoon. And I don't understand you. I don't, I don't."

With horror, she realized that she was starting to cry. "Of course I know that Richard gambled! But is being the wife of a gambler so bad that his own family should reject me, insult me—"

Her voice broke. She searched futilely in the pocket of her voluminous skirt for a handkerchief. "Here," Clive said, and thrust a folded square of linen into her hand. She unfolded it, dried her face, and blew her nose. "Thank you. I'll launder it and return it to you. I mean, I'll *have* it laundered." She added waspishly, "Or is it considered permissible for ladies in this household to do a little light laundry?"

He didn't answer that. He was looking at her, a complex expression in his dark eyes— puzzlement and wariness and just a hint of remorse. He said, "Maybe you really don't—" He broke off.

"Don't what?"

"It doesn't matter."

She wanted to say, Oh, yes, it does! But she must not say that. He seemed less hostile now. Better not antagonize him any more than she had to. Better to keep her mind on her main objective, which was to stay here in the safety of this house until she could find a way to support herself and her child in reasonable dignity and comfort.

Besides, she had a sudden realization of how she must look with her face tear-stained and her hair streaming. Best to get back upstairs as soon as she could.

She said, in the most dignified tone she could muster, "Thank you. I'll return to my room now."

"Wait! Your hairpins."

She turned back, appalled. What would servants have thought if in the morning they had found dark hairpins strewn over the library carpet?

He had bent over now, picking up the pins. As his half-brother had said, Clive had a cool head.

Eleven

THE NEXT DAY he again came home around four in the afternoon and, after an interval, crossed to the little park where Laura sat. Lily was leaning against her mother's knee, excitedly recounting how a squirrel, crossing her path, had jumped right through the hoop. At the approach of the tall man, she fell silent.

"Good afternoon," Laura said.

"Good afternoon." His dark gaze went to the little girl.

"This is Lily," Laura said. "Lily, this is—" She broke off. Would he dislike being referred to as Lily's uncle? Perhaps. But it would seem absurd to introduce him to his niece as Mr. Parrington. She said firmly, "This is your Uncle Clive."

The blue eyes set in the small upturned face searched his with a child's solemnity. Then she gave a smile that seemed all the more dazzling because of her gravity the moment before. Laura often had observed how that smile enchanted adults. It did not fail this time.

"Hello, Lily." Laura realized it was the first time she had seen his own smile. He looked at the hoop lying on the path. "Is that from the old nursery? If so, I used to play with it when I was your age."

Lily looked dumbfounded. His smile grew broader. "You can't believe that I was ever your age, can you?"

He looked back at Laura. "Are you all right?"

She knew he was referring to her encounter with Justin. "Perfectly," she said, feeling her cheeks grow warm.

He said, "My brother returned to his flat early this morning."

"I thought perhaps he had." Because she had slept late, she had not come down to breakfast until almost nine o'clock. Nevertheless, she had feared she might encounter Justin, but there had been no one at all in the dining room.

Clive said, "I'll see you at dinner." He looked down at the child. "Good-bye, Lily."

"Good-bye." Lily watched him go out the gate and cross the cobblestones toward the house. "Mama, do you think he ever really was six years old?"

"Yes. I wouldn't be surprised if at one time he was even younger."

The group gathered around the dinner table that night was larger than the night before. To Laura's surprise, Lady Parrington had come down to dinner. When Laura had tried to see her that afternoon, she had been told by Cornelia Slate that Lady Parrington was "not well today" and was taking a nap. But here she was now, looking lovely and quite young in a blue gown that matched her eyes.

Perhaps tomorrow, Laura thought, her mother-in-law would feel up to seeing her grandchild.

Cornelia Slate was at the table, too, in a green gown that bared bony shoulders that she would have been wiser to keep covered. And Valerie Lockwood, the Parringtons' two-doors-away young neighbor, was there. Her dress was of ruby-colored taffeta, and in her chestnut hair she wore a small ostrich plume of the same color. In her dress of unrelieved black, Laura felt out of place among these brightly gowned women.

Suddenly she wondered if Lady Parrington had worn mourning for Richard, even for a little while. Certainly she must have wanted to wear a symbol of her grief for a beloved though wayward son. But perhaps the Parringtons had decided that mourning clothes would only keep alive whatever gossip there had been over newspaper stories here in London about Richard's death. Surely there must have been some account of it in the London press. It seemed to Laura terribly sad that Lady Parrington might have wanted to wear mourning but felt it unwise to do so.

Eyes fixed on her plate most of the time, Laura said almost nothing. But she remained alert to the talk eddying around her. Valerie Lockwood, seated between Sir Joseph and Clive, was easily the most animated person at the table. Her manner to Sir Joseph, although friendly, was respectful. Her remarks to his son, though, were lightly mocking, conveying a sense that they had long been on familiar terms.

Suddenly, Laura felt someone looking at her. She lifted her eyes and met Clive's intent, almost somber gaze. As their eyes held, she felt something stir within her, an emotion she thought had died with her husband. Quickly she looked down at her plate.

A few moments later she realized that Valerie must have observed that silent exchange between her and Clive. Valerie's voice had become even more animated and mocking, more proprietary. She was describing a ball that apparently had been held sometime during the Christmas season. "And would you believe it, Sir Joseph, your silly son here gave poor Tony Blaine a look that had him shaking in his boots, just because Tony claimed that the second waltz was his."

So that was the way it was. Clive was Valerie's property, or at least Valerie wanted to give that impression. Laura, who had hoped that this young woman of about her own age might become her friend, thought ruefully, You needn't worry about me. Just having been married to his brother seems to disqualify me in Clive Parrington's eyes, no matter what he might have felt about me otherwise.

When the table had been cleared for dessert, Lady Parrington said apologetically, "Do forgive me, all of you, but I think I had best go upstairs now." She looked at Valerie. "Will you come in to see me for a few minutes before you leave?"

"Of course."

As Lady Parrington got to her feet, so did the tall and ungainly Cornelia. A few minutes later, when she had finished her dessert, Laura too asked to be excused. As she rose to her feet, she saw unmistakable relief in Valerie's face.

Half an hour later, while Laura was preparing Lily for bed, she heard a door down the hall open and then close. Probably Valerie was seeing Lady Parrington. Laura imagined Valerie saying something like, "Do you think your daughter-in-law will be staying with you long?" And Lady Parrington might be replying, "My dear, I sincerely hope not. The upset of having her and the child here is

116

more than my nerves can stand. Some other arrangement will have to be made."

As Laura's pulses speeded up, she warned herself again that indignation, openly expressed, was a luxury she could not afford. She must wait patiently for the change that, she was sure, would take place as soon as Lady Parrington laid eyes on Lily.

As on the night before, Bessie came in with a mug of cocoa while Laura still sat at the dressing table. She insisted on taking over the hairbrush.

Laura said, looking at Bessie's freckled face in the mirror, "Does Miss Lockwood dine here often?"

"Oh, lots. A great favorite of both Sir Joseph's and her ladyship's, she is. And of Mr. Clive's, of course."

"Really?"

"Oh, yes. Mrs. Mockton says it just can't be much longer before he pops the question."

To Bessie the prospect was exciting indeed. The whole staff would be asked to the wedding. And afterward they would hold their own celebration in the servants' hall, with Sir Joseph's man James playing the fiddle for dancing, and perhaps the newlyweds coming down to join them in a waltz—

Then a new idea made her suspend the brush above the dark head for a moment. Why was Mrs. Richard asking about Miss Lockwood and Mr. Clive? Could it be that she fancied him for herself?

Instantly she found the prospect of a marriage between Miss Lockwood and Mr. Clive less dazzling than before. How much more romantic if he married Mrs. Richard, after a courtship right here under this roof.

"Not everything Mrs. Mockton says is gospel, though," Bessie said, brushing away. "Personally, I don't think Miss Lockwood will get him. He's thirty-three now. Seems to me he should want someone more experienced-like."

Looking at the reflection of that freckled, earnest face, Laura felt wryly amused. If she read Clive Parrington correctly, it was not what he might "want" that would determine his actions. It was what he chose to allow himself, and that, she felt sure, would not include his half-brother's widow. But of course Bessie couldn't know that, any more than Valerie Lockwood could.

"I think that's enough brushing for now. Thank you, Bessie, and good night."

Twelve

INCREDIBLE AS IT seemed to her, three days later neither of Laura's parents-in-law had exchanged a word with their grandchild. This, even though Lady Parrington had been well enough to come down to the dining room each night.

Every day Laura had hoped that one or both of Lily's grandparents would express a desire to see her, but they did not. Nor did either of them climb the flight of stairs to the servants' floor. That shabby but cheerful nursery might have been on a different continent, as far as the elder Parringtons were concerned. And when Laura led her daughter down two flights of stairs to the front door each afternoon, the other doors along the corridors stood closed, and the corridors themselves were empty except for perhaps a servant or two.

Clive Parrington was the only family member who seemed aware of the child's existence. Each afternoon, soon after he arrived home from the shipping line offices, he would cross to the park. After greeting his niece, he would hold a brief, stilted conversation with Laura.

During those few minutes the attraction—and the tension—between them was almost palpable. It was in their eyes, meeting briefly only to look away. It was in the tones of their voices as they discussed some inconsequential topic like the weather, or the blossom-heavy ornamental cherry tree a few feet away, or the progress of a crew of workmen repairing the cobblestones at the far end of the square. She could imagine him each morning deciding to seek no private conversation with his brother's widow, only to find himself drawn to the little park only a few hours later. As for her, it was with mingled anxiety and anticipation that she saw him cross the cobblestones to the gate each afternoon, and it was with mingled regret and relief that, minutes later, she watched him walk back across the square to the house steps.

She wondered if Valerie Lockwood observed those brief meetings. Almost certainly she did, since her house was only two doors away from the Parringtons'. As for Clive's stepmother, the windows of her rooms did not overlook the square. Just the same, it was unreasonable to think that she was not aware of those meetings. The whole household must be. Certainly Bessie was. Not that she said so. But her awareness was plain in her arch smiles as she stood brushing Laura's hair each night.

Toward the end of the week, around two in the afternoon, Laura sat in her usual place on one of the park benches. She had a volume from the Parringtons' library, George Eliot's *Adam Bede*, open in her lap. Lily, playing with another toy from the nursery cupboard, a jumping jack, sat on the grass several yards away.

"Lady!" The cockney voice made the word sound like *lyedy*. "Mum!"

Startled, Laura looked at the gate. Out on the sidewalk stood a figure that looked more like a bundle of old clothing than a woman. A gnarled hand, obviously dirty even from that distance, but incongruously clad in a black lace mitt, reached through the bars, beckoning. Reluctant and yet strangely drawn, Laura laid her book aside and walked to the fence. She said, making no move to unlock the gate, "What is it you want?"

On her straggly gray hair the woman wore a battered straw hat, ornamented with roses of faded pink cloth. The old face below was seamed with dirt. But the light blue eyes in that ruined face were incongruously bright. She said, "Just to have a look at you, dearie." Because she dropped her aitches, the word *have* came out *'ave*. "Or Mrs. Parrington, I should say." A cackle of laughter revealed that she had a missing front tooth.

Obscurely frightened now, and aware of the strong odor of some sort of alcohol—gin, probably—Laura asked, "Who are you? How do you know my name?"

"Why, I'm her mother."

"Whose mother?"

"*Her* mother. You must know about her, you being married to him and all."

Laura's stomach seemed to tighten. Here it was again, someone's assumption that she had knowledge that she did not in fact possess.

"They pays me not to talk about it," the woman went on. "Pays me well. A pound every month." Again she cackled. "But it's all right to talk to you. I wanted to see what you look like. Know how I knew you was here?"

Laura threw a quick glance at Lily. Thank the lord she was still absorbed in her toy. She looked back at the woman. "How did you know?"

"A girl what's in service with the

Parringtons. She's friends with a girl what's in service with some other people, and her grandmother is a friend of mine. That's how I heard."

A dirty hand suddenly grasped Laura's sleeve. Revolted at the touch, and yet temporarily paralyzed, she stood motionless.

"Did he talk about it to you much, over there in America?"

"I don't know what—"

"Bleedin' shame, that's what it is." Suddenly she was tearfully indignant. "Some people, just because they're rich—"

"Here, here!" Mesmerized by the woman, Laura had not been aware of the constable's approach. But there he stood, tall and ginger-moustached and threatening.

"Take your hand off the young lady."

The soiled hand released Laura's sleeve. The woman said in a whining voice, "I wasn't doing no harm."

"The likes of you don't belong in this neighborhood. Now hop it, before I take you in charge."

The dirt-seamed face, no longer tearful, gave Laura a slyly conspiratorial look. Then, with surprising speed, she turned and scurried away.

"Begging, was she, ma'am?"

Laura said, after a moment, "Yes."

"We try to keep people like her out of neighborhoods like this, but we can't be everyplace."

"Of course not. Thank you, constable."

He saluted and moved away. On legs that felt weak she walked back to the bench and sat down. She felt profoundly repelled, not so much by the woman's appearance or by the alcohol fumes wafting from her as by something else. Standing face to face with her, Laura had felt that there was a person so corrupt that she was scarcely human.

How could that horrible creature have ever had anything to do with the handsome man Laura had loved, the man who had fathered their exquisite child? And yet apparently he had.

She went on sitting there, too abstracted by her bewilderment and nameless fear to be aware when Clive unlocked the gate. A second or more passed before the metallic sound registered on her consciousness. By that time, Clive had almost reached her. So had Lily, racing up the path, her jumping jack abandoned on the grass.

Clive smiled at the child's enthusiastic greeting and smoothed the lemon-colored hair with a long hand. Then Laura said, "Go back and play with your jumping jack, Lily. Your uncle and I want to talk."

Lily looked crestfallen for a moment but then turned and ran away down the path. His eyes suddenly alert, guarded, he asked, "What is it?"

"An old woman, a dreadful woman." Laura's voice shook slightly. "She came to the gate and beckoned me over to her."

"What woman?"

"I don't *know*. She didn't give her name."

He said, after several seconds, "What did she look like?"

"Awful. Dirty and ragged and with teeth missing. And I think she was drunk. She said she was someone's mother. And she plainly expected me to know what she was talking about."

She stopped, took a deep breath, and then said, "What *was* she talking about? You know, don't you? Don't you?"

"No." Shutters had come down in the dark eyes.

"You do. I know you do!"

"Laura, you're being absurd. Some drunken derelict wanders by and—"

"She didn't just wander by! She knew who I was. She called me Mrs. Richard Parrington. Now how do you explain that?"

Again he was silent for a few moments, and then he said, "Servants' gossip spreads from house to house, all over London. And because of newspaper accounts of Richard's death, his widow is of interest, especially to people like that. The woman might have heard about you almost anywhere. Most likely, though, she heard in some pub that you were staying in Sir Joseph Parrington's house."

The woman herself had indicated that the news had reached her through some sort of servants' grapevine. Unconvinced, Laura cried, "But she said other things! She seemed to be saying that she had a daughter, and the daughter was somehow connected with Richard, and that I should know about it—"

"Laura, I think you ought to go home."

She recoiled as if he had struck her. "Home? To New York, you mean?"

"Yes. If you're going to let a drunken old woman upset you like this, perhaps what you need is a familiar atmosphere."

In her confusion and angry distress, she spoke boldly. "Do you really want me to go home?"

Color showed momentarily on his high cheekbones. Then he said, "I'm thinking of your well-being, and the child's. The family would be pleased to send you regular sums for as long as you considered necessary."

"The way you sent regular sums to Richard?" Suddenly she remembered something else the woman had said. "The way you're paying that woman a pound a month?"

He said coldly, after a long moment, "I don't know what you're talking about. Please excuse me now. I have letters to write."

Thirteen

NEITHER LADY PARRINGTON nor Cornelia Slate came down for dinner that night. Alone with the two men, Laura contributed very little to their conversation about the weather and some new shipping company that was forming and the probable outcome of a Parliamentary by-election in the Midlands. No one mentioned that afternoon's incident in the park. But almost as certainly as if she had overheard their conversation, she knew that Clive had discussed the matter with his father.

Long after she went to bed that night, she lay awake pondering her dilemma. In some ways it might be wiser to leave. If she remained, she might find herself increasingly attracted to a man who, she was sure, would never ask her to marry him. Perhaps she should not only return to New York but also swallow her pride to the extent of accepting Clive's offer. Until she had achieved the ability to earn a decent living for herself and her child, would it be such a disgrace to receive an allowance from her child's rich grandparents?

But no, she wanted to stay here. It would be absurd to leave this house with Lily still not knowing Joseph and Dorothy Parrington. Aside from Laura herself, they were her closest relations in the whole world. In fact, with the exception of the two Parrington sons, they were her only relations. And a child needed kinfolk. Much as Laura loved her daughter, she could not make up to her for the lack of a father, grandparents, uncles, and aunts—all those people who would not only enrich her life but care for her if anything disastrous happened to Laura herself.

And then there was Clive. She felt that she could not expect any closer relationship than their present one. And yet she did not want to give up those brief, strained conversations in the park, or those times at dinner when, for an unguarded second or two, his eyes would hold a look that sent a tingling sensation through her.

The clock on her bedroom mantel had chimed two before she fell asleep.

When she awoke the next morning, the light in the room was so dim that she could scarcely believe the clock's hands, pointing to almost nine-thirty. She went to the window and looked out.

The world had been swallowed up by a gray mist. Nothing was visible in the garden below, neither large objects like a Chinese mulberry tree and the white summerhouse, nor bright ones like the reflecting ball on its marble stand.

The door to the adjoining room was closed. Even before she opened it and looked at her daughter's empty bed, she knew what had happened. Bessie, getting no response to her light tap, had concluded correctly that Laura was still asleep. She had gone into Lily's room from the hall and, after closing the connecting door, had dressed the child and taken her upstairs.

Laura climbed to the nursery, where her daughter was finishing breakfast and where Bessie, standing beside the window, remarked that the fog was "a real pea-souper." On her way to the dining room downstairs,

Laura met Mrs. Mockton, who told her that Sir Joseph had just phoned. He and his son had reached their offices before the fog grew too thick, but unless it lifted considerably they would not attempt coming home that night. Instead they would stay at their club.

After her solitary breakfast Laura went back to her room and, by gaslight, began to make minor repairs in her own and Lily's wardrobes. She tightened a button on Lily's blue coat, mended a hem on one of her own petticoats, and threaded fresh blue ribbon through the eyelets of a camisole. Usually such tasks soothed her. But today, perhaps because of her inner conflict as well as the gray smother pressing against the window panes, she grew steadily more restless.

By one-thirty she had finished her solitary meal in the dining room. Her sense of oppression had sharpened to the point where she felt that, fog or no fog, she had to escape this house for at least a few minutes.

She went up to the nursery, where Lily was busy with crayons and an old coloring book Bessie had unearthed from the cupboard. "I'm going over to the park, Lily. But you'd better not come, not with all this fog."

"I don't want to go," Lily said. "That

gray stuff might get down my throat and choke me."

Laura realized that her daughter had never seen fog, at least not fog like this. "It wouldn't choke you, but you'd best stay in anyway."

She returned to her room and put on her out-of-fashion but still serviceable cloak. In the lower hall the dining-room door stood open. Martha, clearing covered dishes from the buffet, looked up and said, "Why, ma'am! Are you going out on a day like this?"

"Only to sit in the park for a little while."

Martha's expression said more clearly than any words that she thought Sir Joseph's American daughter-in-law was daft. "Well, ma'am, at least you won't be run down by a hansom. Nothing is moving. I haven't heard a wheel turn in the square since early this morning."

Laura went outside and descended the stone steps through grayness that felt damp on her face and filled her nostrils with the sour smell of smoldering coal. She realized that smoke, belching from London's hundreds of thousands of chimneys, must be thickening the smother.

As she cautiously crossed the street, she

could see the damp cobblestones directly at her feet. In time to keep from stumbling, she saw the curb and stepped up onto it. She crossed the sidewalk, found the gate after a moment's groping, and fitted the key into the dimly seen lock. The clanging sound it made as it closed behind her seemed somewhat muffled by the fog. Feet crunching over the gravel, she moved to the bench and sat down.

It was like sitting in a tent about two feet in diameter, walled on every side by sluggishly eddying gray mist. There was something soothing in the silence, the sense of isolation from everything else in the world. She felt herself beginning to relax. Perhaps if she sat here for a while, just letting her thoughts drift, the solution to her problems would come to her. Perhaps it would be like several times when, after a night of vaguely remembered dreams, she had awakened knowing the answer to some question that had baffled her the night before.

Dreams. Why was it that one's most vivid and exciting dreams seldom struck others as being so? She recalled recounting to Richard a marvelous dream in which she had been a circus clown, only to realize, as she told him of her argument with a lady bareback rider,

132

that his eyes had begun to glaze over. "You think my dream is *boring*," she accused, and he had answered apologetically, "I'm afraid it does bore me a bit."

Richard. Those Sundays with Richard and Lily in Central Park. Before that, the times during her pregnancy when, even though it might have been ten at night, he had gone out to an ice-cream parlor to buy a pint of vanilla for her. Still earlier, those exciting and yet guilt-ridden nights when she had sneaked out the window to meet the young Englishman who had come so unexpectedly into her life.

And before that, summers when, with the Harmons, she had traveled from one town to another, sitting on the platform while Uncle Benjamin pounded the pulpit, and sweaty-faced worshipers cooled themselves with palm-leaf fans stamped with the name of somebody-or-other's funeral parlor, and white cabbage moths flew in circles around the lanterns hanging from the ridge poles.

Sounds. Lost in memories of long-ago nights on Long Island, Laura for a moment did not identify that metallic creak as the opening of the gate, that crunching sound as a step on the gravel path.

She turned her head. The fog had thinned

somewhat as she sat dreaming. She could make out the gate now, standing slightly ajar. But she could see no one.

Was Clive Parrington somewhere nearby? Had he managed to get home in spite of the fog? But why had he stepped off the path onto the grass? There had been just two crunching footsteps, then silence.

"Clive? Is that—"

The blow came from behind and a little to her right. She knew only an instant's blinding pain before she lost consciousness.

"Ma'am? Ma'am?"

She opened her eyes. The fog must have grown even thinner, she thought confusedly, because she could see him quite clearly as he knelt beside her, the chin strap of his helmet partially hidden by his drooping moustache. But why was she lying on the grass?

The constable said, relief in his voice, "That's better, ma'am! Think you can put your arm around my neck? Tha-a-at's right. Here we go."

He lifted her and carried her through the gate and across the cobblestones.

Fourteen

SHE MUST HAVE lost consciousness again a few moments after that because when she next became aware of her surroundings, she was lying on the bed in her room. Faces loomed over her—Mrs. Mockton's, Cornelia Slate's, Martha's. After that, there was another period of blankness. When she next awoke, somehow knowing that this time she would retain consciousness, it was night. The soft glow of gas jets on either side of the door filled the room. The hands of the mantel clock indicated a few minutes past eight. A man in a frock coat stood, back turned, at the washstand across the room, pouring water from the pitcher into a basin.

Puzzled by his presence and by the fact that she lay fully clothed atop the coverlet, she watched him while he washed his hands and dried them on one of the linen towels hanging on the rack. When he had replaced the towel—neatly, she noticed—she said, "Who are you?"

He turned around, a blond man of about thirty with a small pointed beard and a pleasant smile. "So you're awake." He walked over to the bed and, still smiling, looked down at her. "I'm Dr. Malverne. How do you feel?"

"My head aches."

"No wonder. But fortunately, you have only a slight concussion."

She remembered then that he, or someone, had held a candle backed by a metal reflector close to her eyes. There had been someone else in the room then: Clive Parrington, standing at the edge of the candle glow on the other side of the bed, his face white.

She reached up and touched her head. A piece of bandage had been affixed to an area above and slightly behind her left ear.

Dr. Malverne said, "I'm afraid I had to cut off some of your hair. But you have so much of it that you ought to be able to dress it to hide the spot."

She thought, still groggy, What a nice man. Surely few doctors would even be aware of a woman patient's distress over a missing swatch of hair, let alone feel a need to apologize for it.

She asked, "What happened to me?"

He drew a straight chair to the bedside. "You were sitting in the little park in the square when someone, apparently, hit you over the head. From the shape of the wound I would say that he used something like a heavy cane. I'd also say that the blow was meant to stun, not to kill, although of course your assailant could not be absolutely sure of its effect."

She was remembering now. The dampness on her face. The sense of occupying a tiny scooped-out space in a universe of eddying gray mist. The drift of her thoughts, and then the creak of the gate, the crunch of gravel under someone's foot—

Dr. Malverne's hazel eyes had been fixed on her face. "You're beginning to remember, aren't you? Do you have any idea who came into the park?"

"No, I thought it was—"

She broke off. She had been about to say she had thought it was Clive Parrington. But it couldn't have been Clive who struck her down. It couldn't have been.

Unless he was trying to frighten her into leaving this house? No, she told herself forcibly. Not for that or any other reason would Clive have hurt her physically.

Dr. Malverne said, "You were about to say you thought it was—?"

"When I heard the gate open, I just thought I'd left it unlocked and that it was creaking in the wind. It wasn't until I heard a footstep on the gravel that I realized someone was there. But no, I have no idea who it was."

Seeing sudden skepticism in Dr. Malverne's pleasant face, she realized that the gate could not have creaked in the wind. Fog that dense is virtually windless. But all he said was, "Someone from the police will be here in the morning to talk to you. They'll get to the bottom of it. And I'll be back even earlier in the morning to see if you've recovered sufficiently to talk to the police."

With his right hand he took her wrist and with his left pulled a thick gold watch from his waistcoast pocket. After a few moments he said, "You're doing very well. Your pulse is a little fast, but quite steady. You must have a strong constitution, Mrs. Parrington."

He stood up. "The housekeeper is waiting downstairs. I'll have her send someone up to help you undress."

She cried, with sudden recollection, "My little girl! Is she upset? Where is she?"

"She's fine. Cots have been set up in the nursery, and she'll spend the night there with her nanny. I think the housekeeper called her Bertha."

"Bessie."

"Oh, yes. Bessie. Anyway, the housekeeper told your little girl that you'd had a slight accident—slipped and bumped your head, or something like that—and needed to be undisturbed for a while. I'm sure the child isn't too upset.

"Now I've left you a sedative. It's over there on the washstand. Take it after you're in bed. Well, good night, Mrs. Parrington. I'll see you tomorrow morning."

Mrs. Mockton herself helped Laura undress and brought her a glass of water with which to wash down the pill Dr. Malverne had left. She fell asleep almost as soon as the bedroom door closed behind the housekeeper.

A light tapping awoke her. Hazy sunlight filled the room. She called, just as the mantel clock began to strike eight, "Come in."

It was Martha, with a breakfast tray. When the maid had placed the tray across her lap, Laura thanked her and then said, "How is my little girl?"

"She's fine, ma'am. Mrs. Mockton decided it would be best for her to stay with Bessie until after the police have been here. Miss Slate told me that Lady Parrington wants you to know how sorry she is," Martha went on. "Sir Joseph and Mr. Clive send their regards, too."

"They both came home yesterday?" Again she remembered Clive standing at the edge of the candle glow.

"Yes. They came home about half an hour after the constable carried you here. The fog had pretty well thinned by then.

"I'll be back for the tray in about twenty minutes," she added. "The doctor told Mrs. Mockton that he would be here about eight-thirty."

Left alone with her boiled egg and buttered toast, Laura found that although she felt quite well physically—only a slight throbbing on one side of her head—she felt much more troubled than she had the night before. It wasn't until now that she realized fully what had happened. Someone, with whatever motive, had struck her down.

Had it been some demented stranger, someone who, through a rent in the fog, had seen her alone and helpless on that bench? Could it have been that dreadful old woman? The blow, Dr. Malverne had said, had not been extremely hard. Perhaps that woman would have been capable of striking it.

Or, she thought sickly, had it been someone from this household? Everyone under the Parrington roof must have been aware of her daily airings in the park. And although she had told only two people, Bessie and Martha, of her intention to go to the park yesterday, they might well have mentioned it to others. It surely must have seemed to them worthy of comment that she should go out on such a day.

When Martha came to collect her tray, Laura thought of saying as she looked up into the plain, middle-aged face, Did you tell anyone yesterday that I was in the park?

But no. Better to let the police ask the servants such questions, in an orderly fashion.

Within a few minutes after Martha's departure, Dr. Malverne knocked on the door and then, at her bidding, came into the room. He took her temperature and her pulse and inquired about how she had slept. Then he asked, "Do you have any clearer idea yet as to who might have attacked you?"

There was a certain self-consciousness in his manner, as if he realized he was encroaching upon matters more properly left to the police.

"No, I have no idea at all. Perhaps if I had been really aware of my surroundings—

but I had been sitting there for I don't know how long, daydreaming."

He nodded. "I know. Fog that thick can induce a trancelike state."

What an understanding man he was!

He went on. "Will you come to see me at three next Thursday afternoon? I'd like to make sure your recovery is proceeding normally. My offices are in Harley Street."

Laura gained the not-unpleasant impression that he would be pleased to see her again for more than medical reasons. "Yes, I'll be there."

"I'll leave my card over on the washstand. By the way, a plainclothesman is downstairs. I'll send him up. Goodbye for now, Mrs. Parrington."

The policeman was a Sergeant Simpson, a large man with graying mustaches and large, almost lugubrious brown eyes, like those of a hound. His accent was new to her, neither the Eton and Cambridge English of Richard and his brothers, nor the Bristol intonation of Sir Joseph, nor the broad cockney of the servants. Perhaps, she thought, he was from somewhere in the Midlands. His questions led her through her story: the creak of the gate, the crunch of gravel, and the blow on the head.

"Had you locked the gate, Mrs. Parrington?"

"I don't know. I've been trying to remember. Usually I do. But I was very upset yesterday—"

She broke off. He waited for a moment. She had the dismayed expectation that he was going to say, "Upset about what?" Instead he said, "If you left the gate unlocked, then anyone could have come in, anyone who saw you there, a woman all alone, and decided to steal your purse."

"But I didn't have my purse. I'd put the park key in the pocket of my cloak."

"But a thief wouldn't know that, would he? Not until after he'd knocked you in the head, and looked around for your purse, and not found it. He probably ran then, leaving you to lie there until the constable saw you."

She felt a wave of relief. How much, much better to believe her attacker had been some stranger.

"Of course," he said, "if you *did* lock the gate, then whoever struck you down must have had a key. I've been talking to Mrs. Mockton about the keys. She says she keeps them hanging in a short hall between the kitchen and the servants' dining room. Seems that there's a half-dozen of them, when they're all there, but they keep getting scattered. For instance, the key you carried yesterday is probably still in the pocket of your cloak. Over the years, Mrs. Mockton says, a lot of keys have just disappeared and had to be replaced. And that's probably true of every household on the square. There really doesn't seem much point in locking that gate at all."

He paused for a moment and then said abruptly, "You say you were upset yesterday. Why?"

She hesitated. Tell him about that dreadful old woman? The Parringtons, she was somehow sure, wouldn't want her to tell the police. Certainly Clive Parrington wouldn't.

"Better to tell me, Mrs. Parrington. It could be important."

Yes, better to tell, at least part of it. The woman might be dangerous. And she had more than herself to think about. She had Lily.

"There—there was an awful old woman who came to the park gate the day before yesterday, when I was in there with my little girl. She called me by name, but I have no idea who she was."

"Describe her, please." When Laura had

done so, he said, "Now tell me what she said."

Laura answered, her voice heavy with reluctance, "She didn't make anything very clear. She said that she was someone's mother—someone she just called 'her'—and that her daughter had had something to do with my husband—" She broke off and then said, "I suppose you know that I was married to Sir Joseph and Lady Parrington's son."

He nodded. "Yes, and I know you're a widow, ma'am. The London papers carried an account of your husband's death."

In his opinion, had Richard been killed in the course of a robbery? Or had he been, as that hateful insurance company claimed, a suicide? The sergeant's face gave her no clue as to his personal opinion.

"Did she say how she learned you were in London?"

"Yes. She said that someone in service in this house had told some other servant somewhere or other, and that the second servant had a grandmother who was a friend of this woman's . . . I—I'm afraid it sounds pretty confusing."

"So it does, ma'am, but I'll talk to the servants, of course. You're sure you can't think of anything else that would help us find this old woman?"

She could have said, You could ask the Parringtons, Clive Parrington in particular. But that, she knew, would be unwise indeed. She would lose all hope that she and Lily could stay here until she found a way to make a decent living for both of them. Afraid that already she had said too much, she shook her head.

"No, I can't think of anything." She paused and then said, "I don't suppose you have talked to Sir Joseph or Lady Parrington about my being attacked."

"Oh, but I have. And Mr. Clive Parrington, too. After the constable carried you into this house, he telephoned the Yard. By the time I got here, Sir Joseph and his son had come home. They were all very distressed, but they had nothing to tell me that would help the Department.

"Anyway," he said, getting to his feet, "I'm sure you were attacked by some would-be thief. A fog like that is a godsend to the criminal elements. They knock someone in the head, rob him, and then run off. And unless they run right into the arms of a bobby, which has happened sometimes, there is almost no chance they will be caught.

Good-bye, Mrs. Parrington. We'll let you know if we learn anything."

Fifteen

ABOUT TEN MINUTES after the sergeant's departure, Bessie brought Lily into the room. With a contraction of her heart, Laura saw that the child looked subdued and frightened, just as she had all those months in New York after her father's death. Laura held out her arms. "Lily, don't look like that! I'm fine."

Relief flooded the small face. She ran to the bed and scrambled up onto it. Jarred, Laura's wound gave a throb, but she didn't mind. She said, "Your silly mama slipped and bumped her head, that's all."

"Silly Mama!" Lily echoed enthusiastically, and gave her mother's cheek a smacking kiss. "Mama, can I—"

"May I."

"May I stay with you for a while this morning? Would you read to me?"

"Very well. Bessie, I'll take care of her the rest of the morning."

"Just as you say, ma'am."

When the door had closed behind Bessie, Laura said, "Go pick out a book." Laura had brought most of the nursery library down to her daughter's room so that they would have a choice of reading matter each night.

The child was still in the other room when someone knocked on the door. Laura called, "Come in," and then stared in surprise at Lady Parrington, her face pale and troubled above the marabou collar of her ice-blue satin dressing gown.

"My dear," Lady Parrington said, "I was so distressed to hear—"

She broke off, her gaze riveted on Lily. The child had halted in the doorway, a book in her hand.

Laura's heartbeats quickened. Here it was, the moment she had waited for, counted upon. She said, trying to sound very calm, "Come in, Lily. This is your grandmother. Come and shake hands with her."

Somewhat timidly, the child walked close to Lady Parrington, dropped a curtsy, and extended her hand. "How do you do?"

Lady Parrington did not take the small hand. Face working, she fell to her knees and caught the child to her, so abruptly that Lily gave a startled cry and dropped the book.

"Oh, Lily! Oh, my darling! I didn't mean to frighten you." She held the child away from her a little and kissed her forehead. Eyes swimming, she turned her face toward Laura. "It's just that I didn't know that she looks so much like, so very much like—"

Laura smiled unsteadily. "Yes, she does, doesn't she?"

"Lily," Lady Parrington said, "would you like to come to my rooms for a while? There are so many things to play with. Little china shepherdesses and dogs and horses, and a clock with a whole tiny band that comes out and marches around every hour. Would you like that?"

Her fright forgotten, Lily smiled her radiant smile. "Oh, yes."

Lady Parrington looked at Laura. "Would you mind if she stays with me for an hour or so? I'll take her up to Bessie when it's time for her dinner."

Mind! "I'm sure Lily would like that. Now, Lily, you'll be careful with all your grandmother's things, won't you."

"Of course she will," Lady Parrington said, but it was obvious that if the child shattered her most precious piece of Dresden, she would consider the loss of small moment.

When the two of them had gone out, Laura leaned back against the pillow. She had won.

Just as she had expected, Lady Parrington's defenses had crumpled at her first sight of the child who looked so much like her beloved son. But why, oh why, had she avoided the meeting for so long?

No matter, Laura thought. She had won. She and Lily would be able to stay here indefinitely. She was sure of it, because Lady Parrington would resist her husband, her stepson, or anyone else who tried to banish her grandchild to the other side of the ocean.

Laura had one more visitor that day. Around five-thirty, when the room was already filling with shadows, Clive Parrington knocked and then called out, "May I see you for a moment?"

Her heart gave a nervous leap. She settled her cream-colored bed jacket of light wool around her shoulders and then said, "Come in."

Leaving the door open, he advanced only a step or two into the room. "How do you feel?"

She looked at the tall figure silhouetted against the glow from the hall, where gas jets already burned. Had he been the one who slipped through that gate into the park?

She couldn't believe it. But perhaps that was partly because, here in this semidarkened room, she could feel the attraction between them like an almost palpable thing.

"I feel quite well, thank you."

Another long, awkward pause. He said, "I'm sorry that happened to you."

"Thank you."

Again he was silent. "Well, good night," he said finally, and went out, closing the door quietly behind him.

During the next few days, while Laura lay in bed, Lily spent many hours with her grandmother. She gave Laura enthusiastic accounts of viewing stereopticon slides, and riding in a carriage with her grandmother through Hyde Park, and sailing a brand-new boat on the Serpentine. Bessie, her nose obviously a little out of joint, reported that Lily had been sharing Lady Parrington's tea, thus spoiling her own supper.

By Thursday, feeling quite recovered, Laura rode in a carriage behind the Parrington coachman's broad back to Harley Street. She climbed the steps of a Georgian house. Beside the entrance was a brass plate bearing several engraved names, including that of Hugh Malverne, M.D. She thought, as she had when she read his card, What a nice name.

His offices were on the ground floor at the rear, overlooking a garden filled with clumps of multicolored iris and maples just coming into full leaf. After she had removed her hat and taken down her hair, he said that the wound was healing nicely. He replaced the small bandage with an even smaller one. As she stood before a wall mirror, pinning her hair into place, she was aware of his covert glances, even though he seemed to be studying some sort of ledger on his desk.

He said, "Please sit down again, Mrs. Parrington." Then, when she was seated opposite him, "I'd like to ask you a question or two. How would you characterize your general health?"

"Quite good. In fact," she added wryly, "sometimes I think it is a little too good."

"Too good?"

"I mean that I seem to have too much energy to remain happily idle. In New York I had my daughter to care for, and shopping and housekeeping, and cooking for the three of us. Now all that has been taken out of my hands.

"And yet," she went on, warming to the subject, "people find it shocking that I should consider gainful employment. When I mentioned it to Lady Parrington, she made it clear that it was quite out of the question."

Those pleasant hazel eyes studied her. "What sort of employment did you have in mind?"

"The only skill I have, outside of the ones involved in housekeeping, is needlework. But I'm really quite good at embroidery as well as ordinary dressmaking."

He made a little tent of his fingers—doctor's fingers, well-scrubbed and well-manicured—and regarded her over the top. "Have you ever thought of doing volunteer work, Mrs. Parrington, teaching your skill to others?"

"Others?"

"Working women. Women whose pay, sometimes as little as four shillings a week, won't even buy adequate food for themselves and their dependents, let alone decent clothing." He spoke in a matter-of-fact tone, but she could sense emotion behind his words. "Skill with a needle might enable them to dress better and to keep their clothes in better repair. And then more of them might retain enough self-respect so that—"

He broke off. She said, "I don't understand."

There was a slight flush in the neatly

bearded young face. "Thousands of these girls become fallen women. I hope I don't shock you, Mrs. Parrington, when I say that sometimes I wonder that many more of them don't. It seems to me that a young woman must be virtuous indeed if she resists the money to be made from vice and instead works long hours in a match factory, say, risking, among other diseases, phossy-jaw."

"Risking what?"

"Phossy-jaw. I'm doing research in the field. It's a disease women in match factories develop by inhaling phosphorous fumes. It attacks the teeth and the bones of the jaw and then the vital organs, resulting in disfigurement and often in early death. And their wages, as I have said, can be as little as four shillings a week—this in an industry where stockholders are paid as much as twenty-three percent on their investment."

His flush deepened. "Sorry. I'm afraid I get carried away. But if you would be interested in instructing these girls, I don't think Lady Parrington could object. A number of titled women support the Working Women's League, an organization that concerns itself with London's factory girls. It isn't just so-called agitators like Annie Besant who are trying to change conditions.

"Now I know," he went on, "that the League can always use volunteer office workers in the afternoon. And I'm sure that sewing instruction would be a welcome innovation."

Laura said slowly, "Yes, I think I would be interested." Then, more forcibly, "I know I would."

"Splendid. I'll write out the address for you. And I'll tell Mrs. Riffton you'll be joining her. She's in charge of the League offices." He hesitated and then added, "Its office is in the East End, you know, in a neighborhood of docks and tenements and grog shops. There wouldn't be much point in locating the League in the West End. The girls would feel too intimidated to come to it."

Laura said, remembering that millinery loft, "I've been in slum neighborhoods before."

"Good. The area is quite safe in the daytime. And if you give your needlework instruction in the evenings—and I suppose you'll have to, since these girls are employed in the daytime—I'll be available to escort you back to Bostwick Square. I spend a few hours several nights each week at a clinic near the League offices. That's one of the advantages of bachelorhood. You have more time to devote to activities that interest you."

"I suppose that's true." With an inward smile, she noticed how he had managed to let her know this early in their acquaintance that he was unmarried.

As soon as she returned to the Parrington house, she took off her hat and coat in her room and then went to her mother-in-law's door. Laura had been prepared to meet Cornelia Slate's unfriendly gaze, but apparently she had gone out on some kind of errand, because Lady Parrington's voice called out, "Come in, please."

Laura found her seated in a small armchair in her sitting room, a length of blue lace and a tatting shuttle in her lap. A basket at her feet held a sleeping kitten, rolled into a gray ball.

"You've just missed Lily," the older woman said. "Bessie took her upstairs for her supper."

"I knew she probably had. It's you I want to talk to." Then, looking down at the kitten, "Where did that come from?"

"The Sanford stable." The Sanfords were the Parringtons' next-door neighbors to the north. "Mrs. Mockton knew that the Sanfords had a litter of kittens to give away, and so when I told her that Lily wanted a kitten, she went over there and brought back this one. Lily calls him Fluff. Isn't that a perfect name?"

"Yes." Looking down into her mother-in-law's besotted face, she forbore to add that it was also the name of about half the kittens in the English-speaking world.

"That child is *so* much like Richard." Lady Parrington's voice held that special note, filled with pain and yet loving, with which she always spoke her son's name. "He adored animals."

"I know." Laura recalled how on walks Richard would always linger before pet shop windows, and how he often said it was too bad that their landlord wouldn't let them keep a small dog "for Lily's sake."

"Now sit down, my dear. What is it you wanted to talk to me about?"

When she was seated Laura said, "Dr. Malverne has suggested that I volunteer my services to the Working Women's League. That a place where—"

"I know what it is. Laura, you would be mingling with factory girls! They are not only—coarse. I hear that some of them are—" She broke off.

"I know," Laura said dryly. She wanted to add, And it's little wonder they are.

"I would be there only two or three afternoons or evenings a week. And I understand that many women of the best society are interested in the League."

"That's true. Edith Riffton is prominent in that work, and she is a niece of Lord Lathar's. I hear there are others like her. Well, my dear, perhaps it would be a good idea, if time hangs heavy on your hands."

The capitulation was so sudden and so complete that for a moment Laura was taken aback. Then, seeing a certain gratified shine in the woman's eyes, she felt she understood. With Laura at the other end of London several afternoons and evenings each week, Lady Parrington would continue to have her granddaughter all to herself a good deal of the time.

Sixteen

FOR THE FIRST time in a week, Laura went down to dinner that night. The big room seemed almost crowded. In addition to Sir Joseph and Clive, Lady Parrington and her companion were there. So was Valerie

Lockwood, lovely in green satin. And so was Justin Parrington. A certain look on his handsome young face, half sheepish, half teasing, told her that, drunk as he had been that night, he had remembered their encounter in the library.

Tonight he seemed not only sober but on his good behavior. Well, almost good. Once, under cover of the general conversation, he leaned across the table toward Laura and said in a low voice, "Sorry to hear about that knock on your head."

"Thank you."

"Some would-be purse-grabber, eh?"

"So the police think."

"Not that old crone who grabbed at you through the park gate the day before?"

"When did you hear about that?"

"Oh, I was here one night while you were lying up there with a bump on your head. I took a turn in the square before dinner, and the constable told me about the old woman. Could have been her who did it, you know, or someone connected with her."

There was definitely a small-boy malice in his manner now. Laura said nothing.

"As a matter of fact, it could have been me. I didn't take kindly to being rousted around by Clive on your account." For a moment the look in his eyes was not small-boyish but quite ugly. Then he smiled and said, "Or maybe it was someone else at this table, or in this house. How can you know?"

Laura thought, I won't let him upset me! Things were going well. Lady Parrington was becoming even more attached to her granddaughter than Laura had hoped. She herself had useful, although unpaid, work to look forward to. An attractive man, Hugh Malverne, apparently would not be averse to knowing her better. She wanted to enjoy all that rather than brood over the idea that she might have been struck down by some hidden enemy.

She said coldly, "I prefer to believe what the police say."

He shrugged and turned his attention to the roast beef on his plate.

In the drawing room after dinner, with only a little persuasion from Sir Joseph, Valerie Lockwood agreed to play the piano and sing. "But I'll need someone to turn the pages for me. Clive, would you?"

She chose a French song, one which involved vocal trills as well as several crossings of her left hand over her right, movements that displayed her graceful arms and hands to advantage. Her second song also was in

French. She resisted suggestions that she sing a third song. Then, obviously quite sure that Richard Parrington's American widow neither sang, played the piano, nor spoke French, she shot Laura a triumphant look.

Again Laura thought, If only you knew how small a threat I am to you!

Then her gaze met Clive's. For a moment there was such wretchedness in his eyes, and such longing, that she felt shaken. Quickly the look in his eyes was veiled. He turned away and made some remark to his stepmother.

She was not surprised when, the next night, Clive did not appear at the dinner table. His son was dining at the club, Sir Joseph said. What did surprise and dismay her, as she sat there with her parents-in-law and Cornelia Slate, was how acutely she missed Clive's presence.

She told herself that she must not harbor such emotions. Whatever the barrier between them, he obviously thought it insurmountable, and that of course made it so. Better to keep her thoughts turned in other directions. Thank heaven there had been a little note from Edith Riffton. It said that Dr. Malverne had telephoned and suggested Laura come to the League office the following day.

Early in the afternoon the next day, in an area of London known as Spitalfields, Laura climbed the rickety stairs of a building near the Limehouse docks. At the top of the flight a door stood open. Light poured through very clean windows into a big room. Against its opposite wall a middle-aged woman sat at a flat-topped desk. Near her a younger woman sat at a small table, nimble fingers punching the keys of one of the new type-writing machines. Its clatter was loud in the quiet. Evidently this room also served as a meeting hall, because wooden chairs had been lined up against two walls.

As Laura stood hesitating in the doorway, the older woman got up from her desk and walked across the room. She was a rather plump woman, plainly dressed, with graying brown hair drawn back from a strong, sensible-looking face. She reminded Laura of some of the Long Island farmers' wives who used to appear at the Reverend Harmon's revival meetings. But when she spoke, it was in the accents of an English aristocrat.

"You must be Mrs. Parrington. I'm Edith Riffton. How do you do?"

Laura smiled and returned the greeting.

Mrs. Riffton consulted the small watch pinned to her impressive bosom. "There is someone I must see, a girl who attended our League meetings until she became too ill to do so. She and her family live nearby. Will you come with me? Later I'll show you around this building."

They descended the stairs and emerged into bright, unseasonably warm sunshine that served only to emphasize the squalor of the street. From the windows of tenements, some of which looked near to collapse, issued quarreling voices, infants' cries, and now and then a bawdy or sentimental song. Sidewalk stalls displayed old clothing, secondhand cooking utensils, a side of beef with flies clustered on it. Men and a few women, almost all of them skeletally thin, reeled in and out through the open doors of pubs. Over the cobblestones wagons rumbled, loaded with hogsheads. The air was filled with the smell of drains and decaying wood, and now and then a whiff of alcohol.

Laura thought, Poverty is loud noises and bad smells. Aloud she said, "Some of these people look as if they are starving. Why do they spend money on drink?"

"Perhaps because gin is cheaper than food. In the last century grog shops used to advertise, 'Drunk for a ha'penny, dead drunk for a penny.' A cup of gin costs a little more now but still less than a meal." She added, "Here we are."

They climbed three flights of malodorous stairs. On the first landing a gray-haired woman sat huddled. For a startled moment Laura thought she was the one who had reached through the park gate that day. Then she saw that this woman's blowzy face was considerably younger. They climbed past her. Moments later Edith Riffton knocked on a door.

Shuffling sounds inside. The door opened. Despite the day's heat, the bent woman who stood there wore a ragged dark shawl over her head.

"Good afternoon, Mrs. Coombs. We've come to see Molly."

Apparently too listless even to speak, the woman stepped aside. Laura followed Edith Riffton into the room.

It measured about twelve feet by twelve feet, and it held four people—the shawled woman who had admitted them, a gaunt man of indeterminate age who sat on a wooden box, a baby who lay asleep on a pile of straw in one corner, and a second woman whose age Laura judged to be about forty and who lay on another pile of straw. Her face was disfigured by what might have been a harelip except that it was a raw, angry red.

Edith Riffton asked, "How are you feeling today, Molly?"

The woman said something unintelligible and then tried to smile. With horror Laura saw that although the woman seemed to have no teeth, there was something that gleamed whitely in her mouth. Apparently the upper gum had been eaten through in one spot, showing the bone beneath.

Averting her sickened gaze, Laura took in more of the room's details. A plank spanned two more wooden boxes. Evidently that was the table. In one corner, another heap of straw, which no doubt served the man and the older woman as a bed. In another corner, a charcoal brazier. Appalled, she thought of what this room must be like when charcoal fumes were added to its already fetid atmosphere.

She had been aware of Edith Riffton's voice speaking quiet, soothing words. Now Mrs. Riffton said, "We must go, Molly, but I'll come here again soon." She turned to the shawled woman and pressed what looked like a silver crown into her palm. The woman smiled. It wasn't until then that Laura realized that she was middle-aged rather than old.

She did not speak as she followed Mrs. Riffton down the stairs and past the huddled woman on the landing. But when they were out on the street and heading back toward the League headquarters, Laura said, "She's dying." It was a statement, not a question.

"Yes."

"Can't anything be done?"

"No. The poisoning has attacked her vital organs."

"Isn't there *ever* any cure?"

"For phossy-jaw? Not as yet. Now the only cure is prevention. Perhaps if the match girls worked in well-ventilated factories or wore masks to filter out the phosphorous fumes—"

Laura cried, "Then why don't they?"

"Because it would cost the factory owners money to equip the girls with masks, let alone supply better ventilation." She had been speaking calmly, but now her rage and scorn broke through. "And it costs them nothing to replace a dead or dying girl. There are always a half-dozen other ones eager to earn that three to six shillings a week."

They passed an open doorway with a sign above it, FOUR LEAF CLOVER MUSIC HALL. From inside came the sound of someone playing a bucolic ballad, "We Will A-Maying Go," on an out of tune piano.

Laura asked, "Is that baby Molly's?"

"Yes. He's six months old."

"How old is Molly?"

"She's almost eighteen."

Laura said nothing more until they entered the League building. Then she leaned her head against the wall and burst into tears. "I'm sorry," she said brokenly, "but I never knew there could—I know a little about poverty in New York, but I never saw or even heard of anything like this."

Edith Riffton said, "Well, now you have. I'll walk with you to the Tower Bridge. You can hire a hansom there to take you home."

"Home!" Astonishment checked her tears. "But you were going to show me where I'll teach my classes."

Mrs. Riffton said after a long moment, "You mean you still want to work for the League?"

"Of course! Now more than ever."

Edith Riffton's gaze studied Laura's tear-stained face. "I'm afraid I owe you an apology, Mrs. Parrington. To put it bluntly, I thought you might be just another young woman trying to curry favor with Dr. Malverne."

"Curry favor!"

"Yes. He's a fine man, and the League is grateful for his interest in us. But he's also an attractive young bachelor. Quite a few pretty young women, knowing of his enthusiasm for the League, have volunteered their services. I've spent considerable time and effort trying to teach them to be useful here, only to have them discover that they are too sensitive to work with slum girls. It's a discovery they make at about the same time as they discover that they have not awakened Hugh Malverne's romantic interest.

"I wanted to make sure you were not another such one," she went on. "That's why I took you to see Molly Coombs. I felt that if your main interest was the doctor, you would decide that there must be an easier way of trying to attract him. I do apologize, Mrs. Parrington."

Laura wiped her cheeks with a handkerchief and then smiled. "Your apology is accepted. And now may I see where I'll be teaching my class?"

She returned to the Parrington house in the late afternoon. Just as she was about to enter her room, the door to Lady Parrington's rooms opened and Valerie Lockwood stepped out into the hall. "Why, hello!" she said in a bright voice and walked to where Laura stood. "Lady Parrington tells me you're joining the Working Women's League."

"Yes, I've just come from there."

"So, so brave of you! I would never have the courage even to go into a neighborhood like that."

Her suspicion aroused by Valerie's unwontedly friendly manner, Laura smiled but said nothing.

"I don't imagine," Valerie went on, "that you'll be visiting the places of entertainment in the East End."

"Places of entertainment?"

"Music halls. Women of our sort don't go to such places, of course, but some men do, particularly young men from the universities. I hear that a place called Billy Barker's is especially popular."

Still puzzled, Laura said, "It is?"

"You've never heard of it? I thought surely Richard must have mentioned it to you. He used to go there so often."

So that was it. She hoped to wound with some revelation about Richard. "He did?"

"Yes. I heard that his favorite entertainer, a singer named Belle Mulroney, is still there."

She said, as if the idea had just occurred to her, "You know, perhaps you should contrive to make her acquaintance. You might find that you and she have a lot in common. Well, I must be leaving. But so nice to have had a little chat with you."

As Valerie moved toward the landing, it seemed to Laura that even her back looked triumphant. Laura felt mingled annoyance and pity. How absurd of Valerie to think that she could be hurt by the revelation that Richard had bedded down with some music hall singer. She had never been under the impression that until their marriage Richard had lived like a monk.

If only she could say to Valerie, "We're not really rivals, you know. Even if I tried, I couldn't stand between you and Clive Parrington."

But such healthy frankness was permitted only to men. Convention decreed that two women attracted to the same man should veil that fact with silken smiles, all the time stabbing at each other with words like tiny knives.

As she opened the door to her room, Laura thought, When we're forbidden to express openly some of our strongest emotions, it's no wonder that so many of us have nervous ailments.

Seventeen

LAURA FOUND HERSELF increasingly caught up
in League activities. Two afternoons each
week she reported for office duty. While the
typist, a paid employee, worked at her clattering machine, Laura sat with Edith Riffton
and another volunteer or two at the big desk,
toting up figures in the League's ledgers or
composing pleas for funds from individuals
and organizations. Three evenings a week, in
a smaller room, Laura taught her sewing
classes. Under her direction, young women
who had never held a needle learned to re-
furbish for their own use or that of their
children the clothing donated to the League.
They mended tears, replaced missing buttons, shortened or lengthened hems, took
waists in or let them out. After a while she
began to teach them to work from paper
patterns. Thus a blue velvet evening cloak,
donated by a steel manufacturer's wife, became a warm jacket for an eighteen-year-old
mother and coats for her two-year-old twin
daughters.

Observing the clumsy, work-roughened
fingers and the missing teeth that might or

might not signal the first onslaught of the dreaded phossy-jaw, Laura wondered that they could laugh, tell jokes, and tease each other about their sweethearts. It must be, she decided, that Nature equipped young people with high spirits that not even grinding toil nor the threat of disease could subdue, at least not until they were past twenty.

Her first evening at the League, when she descended from the offices to the street, she found Dr. Malverne waiting for her in a hansom cab. In answer to her protest that he was being too kind, he said, "It's as I told you. I'm in attendance at an evening clinic in this neighborhood. It will be no trouble at all for me to make sure that you get home safely."

After that he was always there, ready to escort her back through evening light that steadily lengthened as the summer solstice approached. At his request, the cabbie would take them along the Embankment, where the river gleamed like iridescent silk in the after-sunset light, and where the handsome new electric standard lamps stood ready to bloom in the dusk. Laura enjoyed not only the beauty of those drives but Hugh Malverne's conversation, too. If encouraged, he would talk of his work, but mostly he talked of the reform movement that, in this next-to-the-last decade of the nineteenth century, seemed to be sweeping all of Europe, London included.

"As a matter of fact, the reform movement is late in reaching London. The horrible conditions in the coal mines in the Midlands are already much improved. I don't know whether you heard about it in America, but English mine owners employed children—mostly girls, since they tend to be smaller—to drag ore cars through the low-roofed tunnels. They worked almost totally unclothed because of the heat, and they worked on all fours, with a harness that attached them to the cars. Because they were denied sunlight and fresh air in their growing years, many of them were very much stunted. When the Queen set up her Inquiry Commission—and God bless her for it—they found young women of eighteen or twenty who were the size of eight-year-olds. Many of them had never—" He checked himself and then said, "Many of them had never matured. But female children no longer work in the coal mines. Now it's time to do something about the London poor, including the girls who work in the match factories."

His voice quickening with excitement, he

told of how he had taken part in the gigantic reform rally in Trafalgar Square more than six months before. Among the hundred thousand demonstrators had been the artist William Morris and a young music critic named George Bernard Shaw.

"But the important thing," he said, "is that working men and women by the tens of thousands were there. I think it has been made plain to London employers that they can no longer buy off half-starved people with a contribution to the Lord Mayor's unemployment fund."

During those rides through the late spring twilight, he did not try, by look or word or gesture, to make love to her. She wondered if it was because he had no desire for more than her friendship. Perhaps. But she thought it more likely that he, an outspoken liberal politically, was in other respects a highly conventional man—much more so, say, than Clive Parrington. And conventional men don't make advances to widows still in mourning dress.

Except for those two afternoons a week when she did office work for the League, she continued to take Lily to the little park in the square each day. And she managed to take her there alone, despite Lady

Parrington's hints that she too sometimes sat in the park "during the warmer months." Her grandmother had Lily with her in her rooms for many hours each week—so many, in fact, that Bessie now spent more time on her former "jooties" than in the nursery. It was only right, Laura felt, that she should have her little girl all to herself for a number of hours each week.

Often as she sat in the park she saw Clive Parrington come home and climb the steps. Each time, with mingled hope and apprehension, she wondered if he would turn and walk across the cobblestones to the park. Instead, without a glance in her direction, he would go into the house and close the door. Even on those afternoons when he came home, he was likely as not to be absent from the dinner table. And when he was there he remained silent for long stretches of time, leaving it to others to carry on the conversation.

Laura wondered if Valerie Lockwood was aware that Clive no longer entered the park when she and Lily were there. Surely she must, since the park gate was visible from her own house. Did Valerie take heart from the knowledge? Laura had no way of knowing. She had not seen the other young woman at the Parrington dinner table or anyplace else since that afternoon when they had encountered each other in the upstairs hall.

Every now and then Laura thought of that brief verbal exchange. And as time went on she began to think more and more about Belle Mulroney, someone who was just a name to her but who apparently had been considerably more than that to Richard. It was not that she began to suffer belated pangs of jealousy. But she did wonder if the music hall singer was in any way connected with that old woman who had reached a dirty, lace-mitted hand through the park gate that afternoon.

Then one night in her sewing class one of the girls, a blonde named Nancy, mentioned Billy Barker's. Her sweetheart, it seemed, had "won ten bob." She didn't say at what; Laura hoped it wasn't a dog fight. Anyway, he had treated her to an evening at Billy Barker's.

As each girl was folding up her work and placing it in one of the wooden boxes arranged along one wall, Laura said to Nancy, "What is this Billy Barker's?"

"A music hall, ma'am. It's ever so much fun. Toffs from the West End come there sometimes. Gentlemen, of course, not ladies."

"Where is it?"

"Not far from here, on Bengali Street." Then, uneasily, "But I don't think it would be to your taste, ma'am. I mean, if you're thinking of having some gentleman take you there—"

"I'm not. It's just that I think I heard something about an entertainer there, someone named Belle Mulroney. Does she still sing there?"

"Oh, my, yes! She's been there for donkey's years. She's old, of course. Must be thirty-five, or near it. But she's good at comical songs, like 'Sailing with My Sailor, Over the Salty Sea.' Have you heard that song, Mrs. Parrington?"

"No. Perhaps they never sing it in America." Laura turned away.

Nancy felt puzzled. Now why would the likes of Mrs. Parrington be asking after the likes of Belle Mulroney? Could it be that some toff Mrs. Parrington fancied could be hanging around Belle? No, that didn't seem likely, not with Mrs. Parrington being so pretty and Belle so long in the tooth. Nancy shrugged the question away. She liked the League ladies, but she'd never been able to figure them out—coming to a place like Spitalfields, for instance. *She* wouldn't spend ten minutes in the neighborhood if she didn't have to.

Half an hour before she was due at the League office the next afternoon, Laura hesitated before a tall brick tenement on Bengali Street. A door to a narrow passageway stood open. Above it a painted wooden sign, creaking in a slight wind that blew down the dirty street, showed the top-hatted head of a grinning fat man. Below were the words BILLY BARKER'S.

She went a yard or so down the passageway, hesitated in a wide doorway to her right, then advanced a few steps into a large room with windows facing the street. Round tables, now unoccupied, took up most of the floor space. Along one wall was a long counter, over which, probably, drink was served. At the far end of the room, parted curtains of frayed red velvet revealed a stage. Its backdrop, with painted balconies leaning close over a canal where a gondola floated, obviously represented Venice. At a square table near the opposite wall sat a fat man with a vague resemblance to the picture on the sign outside. Daylight coming through the windows fell on the outspread ledger before him.

"Mr. Barker?"

Billy Barker thought, not getting to his feet, Blimey, what's she doing here? A lady by the look of her, and in mourning clothes!

"That's right, ma'am." His smile did not alter the shrewd watchfulness of the small gray eyes in the fat face. "Billy Barker, at your service."

"My name is Mrs. Parrington. I'm a member of the Working Women's League."

So she was one of the reformers. Well, he had no objections to some things they did. It was fine with him if they got wages raised. The lads and the girls deserved it, and besides, it would give them money to spend in his place. What he objected to was the crazy notions some of them talked about, like votes for women. And this business about reforming the street walkers. What business of theirs was it if a girl decided to take to the streets instead of the factories? At least he'd never met a tart with phossy-jaw, no matter what else they might have.

"Pleased to know you, ma'am. What can I do for you?"

"I thought that perhaps you could give me

the address of an employee of yours, a Miss or Mrs. Belle Mulroney."

The little eyes narrowed. "Something wrong, ma'am? I hope Belle isn't in no kind of trouble. She's a good girl. I can vouch for her."

"Oh, there's no trouble. It's just that we once had a—a friend in common, and so I'd like to see her, if possible."

A friend in common. That didn't seem likely. But at least this Mrs. Parrington didn't look like a troublemaker.

"She lives right here, ma'am. One flight up, first door at the head of the stairs."

She thanked him, walked back along the passageway, and climbed narrow and splintered stairs. The door just off the landing was closed. She knocked, and a woman's voice called, "Come in!"

Opening the door, Laura was met by a mingled odor of talcum powder, perspiration, and singed hair, the latter predominating. An instant later she saw why. Back turned, a woman in a camisole and petticoat sat at a dressing table, holding a curling iron to a gas jet that flamed beside the mirror. Looking surprised, she placed the iron on a metal stand on the dressing table, then stood up and turned around.

"And who might you be?" The tone was not challenging, merely curious. She was a tall woman, Laura saw, not fat but big, wide of shoulder and bosom and hip. Her obviously dyed hair was reddish-blond, her features large but symmetrical, and her greenish eyes friendly. She appeared to be somewhere in her midthirties.

"Miss Mulroney?"

"Well, yes. Not that anybody calls me that. People call me Belle." Laura noticed that her accent, like her name, was Irish.

"I'm Laura Parrington."

"Glad to—" She broke off. "Did you say Parrington?"

"Yes. I'm Richard Parrington's widow."

"Well, I'll be a son of a gun!" She raised her voice. "Coleen!"

A large girl who looked to be about twelve appeared in the doorway across the room. At once Laura saw that the child must be Belle Mulroney's. Her hair was the reddish-blond shade her mother's must have been before she'd had to resort to the dye pot. Her features were much the same. But the girl's eyes were not hazel. Instead they were blue and wide-set and oddly familiar.

Belle was rummaging around in a soiled-looking reticule of pink satin. She extracted a coin and held it out. "Run down to Midgeley's and get me a packet of Venus Talcum Powder."

"Aw, Mum!" the girl protested. She threw an avidly curious glance at the visitor.

"Now, hop it! And don't stand outside the door listening. If you do, you'll get your ears boxed."

The girl went out. Belle said, "Oh, lord. I forgot my manners. Sit down, sit down."

Laura had become aware that the room must serve as both a theatrical dressing room and a parlor. A metal clothes rack hung with brightly colored costumes stood next to the dressing table. But over in one corner were two ancient wing chairs, flanking a table on which many small photographs were displayed. From a cursory glance, Laura gained the impression that they were all of Belle in various costumes.

She chose one of the chairs, and Belle sat down again on the dressing-table bench. "So you're Richard's widow. I knew he had gone to America, but I didn't know he had a wife and child until it was in the papers. About his death, I mean." She paused and then said, her Irish accent more pronounced than ever, "I was sorry for your trouble."

"Thank you."

"I suppose Richard told you about me and him."

"No." She hesitated, unwilling to explain that another woman had told her out of jealous vindictiveness. "I heard after I joined the Working Women's League." At least so much was true.

"No wonder you heard, the League and Billy Barker's being in the same neighborhood. Now, what did you want to see me about?"

"I was wondering if you'd mind telling me how you and Richard met."

"Mind? Of course not. It was right here. Downstairs, I mean. He came in one night, and between my numbers he offered to buy me a drink, and that led to him coming down here a few more times, and that led to Coleen." She laughed.

"Richard must have been very young when—when you and he—"

"When he and I were having it on? He was twenty, I was twenty-five. Oh! I see how you'd think I was even more of a cradle-snatcher than I was. It's Coleen, ain't it? How old do you think she is?"

"I'd say about twelve."

"She's not even ten yet. Great lummox, ain't she? Going to be bigger than I am.

Well, maybe she can team up with some female acrobats like what Billy Barker had here once. Coleen could be the bottom of the pyramid."

Laura almost gave an appreciative smile but then, seeing that Belle was serious, managed to check herself.

"Too bad she didn't take more after Richard," Belle said. "Just around the eyes, you notice. What a handsome man he was! Of course, as I'm sure you know, he had his weakness."

Laura nodded. "His gambling, you mean. He promised me that once we were married, he'd give it up. But every once in a while—"

Her voice trailed off. Belle regarded her visitor for a long, silent moment and then said, "Well, a lot of young toffs gamble, and some not so young. And he was generous. Gave me a thousand pounds when I told him I was in the family way. Of course, I didn't see him again after that, but then, I didn't expect that I would."

She paused and then added, "Did it upset you, hearing about me?"

Laura said, "Of course not. It all happened before I even met him."

As they sat there in an almost companionable silence, there seemed to be a third person in the room, the father of the sturdy Coleen and the exquisite Lily.

Finally Laura said, "One thing more. One afternoon several weeks ago, an old woman came up to me in Bostwick Square—in the little park there, I mean—and mentioned Richard and then said she was the mother of someone I gathered knew Richard, someone she just called 'her.'"

"I couldn't have been the 'her' she was talking about, luv. My mum and dad are both dead, and even alive they was never once out of Ireland."

"I see. Well, the chances are that the old woman who spoke to me was out of her wits from drink, or age, or both." She stood up. "I must get back to the League office. Thank you for seeing me."

Eighteen

ALL THE REST of that afternoon, while she penned fund-soliciting letters—"so much more effective with some people than type-written ones," Edith Riffton believed—Laura kept thinking of Belle Mulroney and her daughter. Did the Parringtons know about that episode in Richard's life? Had they even contributed the thousand pounds Richard had given to Belle? If so, perhaps that had been the final straw that broke the family's patience. No, that couldn't be. It wasn't until a couple of years after his affair with the music hall singer that his family had banished him to America.

As she sat there, head bent over sheets of letter paper, the typewriting machine clattering behind her, she felt a new surge of anger against the Parringtons. How dare they be so secretive about Richard! She was his widow and the mother of his daughter. She had a right to know everything about him.

When she reached the Parrington house that afternoon, she didn't go straight up to the nursery as she usually did. Instead, after taking off her hat and coat in her room, she descended through the silent house to the library, leaving the door to the hall open behind her. She stood beside the lace-curtained window, a book open but unread in her hand, until she saw Clive Parrington coming along the sidewalk.

After she heard the front door open and close, she called, "Clive?"

He appeared in the doorway, his face both surprised and wary.

"Will you come in here, please, for a moment? And will you close the door behind you?" At this time of the afternoon, three hours before dinner, there was little chance that either of the older Parringtons would appear on the ground floor. Sir Joseph, if not still in his office, would be drinking sherry at his club. Lady Parrington would be in her rooms, taking tea with Cornelia Slate. Nevertheless, Laura wanted to make sure that neither they nor any of the servants overheard her.

Without speaking, Clive stepped into the room and closed the door behind him. Laura replaced the book on its shelf and then said, "Do you know anything about a woman named Belle Mulroney?"

"Who?" For a moment he looked genuinely puzzled. Then his eyes grew even colder. "I remember now. That was the name of a music hall performer my brother was involved with. Did he tell you about her?"

"No. As a matter of fact, Valerie Lockwood mentioned her to me." When he made no reply to that, Laura went on, "Today I saw Belle Mulroney and her child, Richard's child. Tell me, was Belle the reason you and your parents decided Richard had to go to America?"

He said, his face enigmatic now, "That contributed to our decision."

"It did? Odd that you should wait two years before deciding."

His face flushed. He made no answer to that but instead asked, "Where did you see this woman?"

"At Billy Barker's Music Hall."

"You mean you went to that place?"

"Yes. It's quite near the League office."

"That damned League!"

"You don't approve of it?"

"I don't approve of a young woman like you going to a neighborhood like Spitalfields! And not just in the afternoons but three evenings a week."

"I'm quite safe. Dr. Malverne escorts me home."

"I'm aware of that! Confounded reformer. I'll wager he's the one who suggested you join the League. Why doesn't he just attend to his patients' medical needs and outside of that mind his own business?"

She thought, feeling pleased, Why, he sounds jealous. Aloud, she said, "Dr. Malverne believes the London working class is treated abominably. So do I. This is the capital of the largest empire the world has ever known. And yet working people suffer far more here than in Germany, or in the Scandinavian countries, or in America. Do you as an Englishman approve of that?"

"No! Unlike my father, I feel that laboring men and women should be and will be organized. For instance, I hear the match factory girls may go out on strike. If they do, I hope they win. But I also feel it's something in which a woman like you shouldn't be involved."

She looked at him silently. He went on, "You shouldn't be going into that neighborhood at all. Such areas are rife with disease. If you don't care about your own welfare, you ought to care about your child's."

She said, stung, "Don't tell me about guarding my own child!" Then, with an intuitive leap, "Are you really so concerned about my health? Or do you have reason to think that by going to that neighborhood several times each week I might in time get closer to the truth?"

He said evenly, "I have no idea what you are talking about."

"Oh, yes, you do. The truth of why you Parringtons forced my husband out of his own home and out of his country."

"What reason did Richard give you?" His voice was as cold as his face.

189

"That it was solely because of his gambling. But I can't accept—"

"You'd better accept it. It's the only explanation you're ever going to have from Richard or anyone else."

He turned and walked out. After a moment she heard the distant but far-from-gentle closing of his door on the floor above.

Clive was not at the dinner table that night. Laura wondered if, before leaving the house to dine somewhere else, he had told either of his parents about that conversation a few hours earlier in the library. She decided that perhaps he had told Sir Joseph about her visiting Belle Mulroney. But after thinking it over, she felt that it was highly unlikely that he had told his stepmother. In fact, it seemed improbable to Laura that Lady Parrington even knew she had another granddaughter, living above a music hall in Spitalfields. It was the sort of knowledge from which they would have done their best to shield her. Certainly as she chattered away about the engagement of one of the Earl of Darlington's daughters, there was nothing in her face or manner to indicate that she was disturbed.

Immediately after dinner, Laura went upstairs. Lily, who in the past couple of weeks had begun to insist that she was old enough to undress herself, was already in bed, drinking cocoa from her own special mug, which Mrs. Mockton had found somewhere below stairs. Like the one from which Laura drank her own nightly cocoa, it had a light brown glaze on the outside. But at some time in the past someone, probably a nanny with a talent for such work, had drawn a dancing white poodle on it. Around the base of the mug in white letters were the words, THIS MUG IS RICHARD's. Lily loved it.

For twenty minutes Laura read aloud to her daughter from Stevenson's *A Child's Garden of Verses*. Then she went into her own room. When Bessie arrived half an hour later with a mug of hot cocoa on a tray, Laura was in a nightdress and negligée.

As Bessie brushed the luxuriant dark hair, she asked, "Did you go to the Working Women's League today, ma'am?"

Laura took a sip of cocoa. "Yes, as usual."

Bessie did not have much sympathy with the match factory girls and such like. Why didn't they go into service? True, a girl in service was lucky to get six pounds a year above her room and board, and if she was with the wrong sort of people, the room and board were miserable and the work days fifteen hours long. But if a girl was neat and clean and quick, she could get a post with a nice family like the Parringtons. And if, unlike the heroines in *Housemaids' Own*, she didn't get married and had to remain in service until she was too old to work—well, people like the Parringtons never turned a servant into the streets.

Bessie disapproved of Mrs. Richard's recent behavior on still another account. She had been so sure that Mr. Clive was falling in love with the American widow. The night someone had struck her down, he had seemed terribly upset. But since then he'd never even gone over to the park when she was there. She must have said or done something wrong.

Bessie would have felt at least somewhat consoled if Mr. Clive had resumed his attentions to Miss Lockwood. But according to Jane Sims, the Lockwoods' parlor maid, he never even called on Miss Valerie anymore.

It was enough to make a girl lose her faith in romance.

Laura had just finished her breakfast the next morning and returned to her room when someone knocked. She opened the door to see Cornelia Slate standing in the hall. She was dressed for the street in a green coat of lightweight wool, with a green-ribboned straw hat covering her coronet of chestnut braids.

She said, "Good morning." As always when she spoke to Laura, her tone was reserved to the point of reluctance. Laura thought, with a flash of sympathy, How she must hate me! How many nights, Laura wondered, had the woman lain awake, wishing fervently that the American would go back to New York, wishing even more fervently that she herself had not blurted out her old, blasted dream about herself and Richard.

She went on, "If it's convenient, Lady Parrington would like to see you in her rooms now."

"Oh! Of course. I'll be right there."

Cornelia nodded, then turned and walked toward the stair landing.

A few minutes later, at Lady Parrington's bidding, Laura entered that jewel box of a dressing room across the corridor. Seated in a small armchair, Lady Parrington laid her knitting, something that appeared to be a child-size blue mitten, in a basket beside her feet. "Please sit down, my dear." Then, "My husband has made the most marvelous suggestion. I think I've told you that we always spend August at Walmsley."

"Yes, you did." And long before she met her mother-in-law, Richard had told her of how each year in the late summer the

Parringtons had gone to Walmsley, the house about thirty miles south of London built by Dorothy Parrington's great-great-great-grandfather, Clarence Calverton.

"And do you remember how last night at dinner I remarked that Lily looked somewhat thin and pale?"

"Yes, and I said that probably it was because she is growing so fast."

"That may be. Nevertheless, before he left for his office this morning, Joseph told me he believes that she would benefit enormously from a fortnight at Walmsley, and I agree. We could leave, say, three days from tomorrow."

"We?"

"You, of course, and myself and Lily and Cornelia. No need to take Bessie. Surely you and Cornelia and I can look after one small girl! Besides, Mrs. Mockton's rheumatism is bothering her, and she needs all the staff.

"At Walmsley," she went on, "we have a caretaking couple named Sproggs, as well as a coachman and an old man named Zach who is in charge of the stables. I'll write to the Sproggses this afternoon and ask them to hire the village people who always help staff the house when we are there."

She paused, face eager. "Well?"

Briefly Laura wondered why Sir Joseph had suggested just at this particular time that they spend a fortnight in the country. Was it because his son had told him that his daughter-in-law had been talking to Belle Mulroney? Perhaps. On the other hand, Sir Joseph might have been concerned solely with his granddaughter's health and his wife's peace of mind.

Whatever the reason for his suggestion, Laura found that she welcomed it. True, her work with the League seemed to her eminently rewarding. But for as long as she could remember, late spring had brought her a yearning for open country. This was the time of year when, during her girlhood, she had traveled with the Reverend Harmon and his wife from one revival meeting to another along what some people called the Hallelujah Trail, a series of Long Island roads that led through elm-shaded villages and the burgeoning potato fields that separated them. After she and Richard were married, they always managed to take Sunday train rides out to Long Island or up to Westchester during late May and early June. Here in England it would be wonderful to visit the country during that magical time when the lettuce-pale leaves began to take on their deeper summer green and daisies—surely England had daisies—began to star the roadsides and the meadows.

She said, "I think that's a wonderful idea."

Nineteen

THE CARRIAGE THAT had brought them from the railway station, an old but beautifully kept brougham with the Calverton coat of arms on the door, topped a rise in the road. Laura caught her breath. There below, in a cup of low emerald-green hills, was Walmsley.

Late afternoon sun lay warm on its wide, three-story facade of reddish stone, its myriad windows, and its square corner towers. Her ancestors had erected it, Lady Parrington had said, in 1635, and because they had chosen to build in the Tudor style the house looked considerably older than its actual age.

Now that the house was in sight, the matched pair of bay horses drew the carriage at a faster clip down the road and along a circular drive. The coachman reined in where, at the foot of the steps, a couple Laura knew must be the Sproggses awaited them. Both thin and short and gray-haired, they might have been brother and sister rather than husband and wife.

After Lady Parrington introduced her daughter-in-law and granddaughter to the Sproggses, they all climbed the fan of steps to where massive doors stood open. They went into the lower hall. Laura gained a swift impression of beautiful linenfold paneling on the walls, and of a massive Tudor staircase leading upward. At the foot of the staircase other servants awaited them, a stout woman cook and two girls of about eighteen and two men in their early twenties. These apparently were the local people the Sproggses had hired at Lady Parrington's bidding. Shy and awkward-appearing, they obviously lacked the city sophistication shared by all the servants, even Bessie, in the Parringtons' London house. But as they acknowledged Mrs. Sproggs's introductions—the girls with clumsy curtsies, the men tugging at their forelocks—their smiles were warm and friendly.

In the wake of a thin, blond girl named Doris, Laura and Lily climbed the staircase and walked for a hundred feet or so along a wide corridor where oriental rugs lay on the polished floor and gilt-framed portraits, far more numerous than in Lady Parrington's

London sitting room, looked down from the walls. Then they turned onto a narrower corridor. Evidently, Laura noticed, gas had not been laid on at Walmsley. The wall sconces along both the main corridor and this branching one held candles.

As in the London house, she and Lily had been given adjoining rooms. Although these rooms were smaller, they were much more to Laura's taste, with paneled walls and with beds and chests of drawers that, she was sure, had been standing in this room when most of America was still a raw wilderness.

Best of all, from her window in this, the east wing of the house, she could see through a gap in the emerald hills, dotted with sheep, the steeple of a village church.

One of the young men servants brought up their valises. A few minutes later, Doris arrived with a supper tray for Lily. The child was too excited to eat much of her meal and, once she was in bed, was still too restless to settle down for sleep. Laura read aloud from *Alice* for half an hour before Lily's eyelids began to droop and then finally closed.

Laura hurried back along the corridors and down the stairs. Because Mrs. Sproggs had told her where the dining room was—

"to your right at the foot of the stairs"—she had no trouble finding it.

Her mother-in-law was already there, seated at one end of the long table with another place laid close beside her own. Cornelia, she explained, had a headache and had asked to have a tray sent to her room.

"I'm sorry," Laura said. "And I'm sorry I'm late. I had trouble getting Lily to sleep."

"My dear, it's perfectly all right. Do sit down. Now, about Lily. Sproggs tells me that our pony is still alive. Justin used to ride him. Toby is old and he's fat, but that's all to the good, isn't it? We wouldn't want Lily to ride a spirited animal. Not that she will really be *riding*. Zach will just lead the pony around the stableyard."

"Zach?"

"He grooms the few horses we keep here. He's been at Walmsley longer than I can remember. I think I was about four when he came here as a stableboy. He's deaf as a post now, but he's still good with horses." She paused and then asked, "Is Lily still upset about Fluff?"

Even though her mother and grandmother had explained to her that kittens are apt to become sick on trains, Lily had sulked for a while over leaving Fluff behind. "No, she seems too excited over being here to think much about her kitten."

"I do hope that means she'll like being at Walmsley."

"Of course she will! So will I. It's such a beautiful house."

"Yes, isn't it?" Lady Parrington looked around the room, at the mullioned windows through which the last of the daylight filtered, at the massive, silver-laden buffet against one wall, and at the long table, its highly polished surface a reflecting pool for a lighted candelabra of Georgian sterling. There was an oddly bittersweet expression on her still-lovely face, as if she were recalling both happy events and some not happy at all.

Again, Laura wondered at Dorothy Parrington's marriage. Why should she, the beautiful heiress to the Calverton name and this splendid house, have married a merchant seaman's son, no matter how much wealth he had achieved?

One of those love matches that no one except the pair involved can understand? Possibly. Certainly it was easy to imagine plain, humbly born Joseph Parrington falling madly in love with a lovely aristocrat. But that ardor, if it had existed, now was apparently something in the long-ago past. Laura had never observed any unpleasantness between Sir Joseph and Lady Parrington. On the contrary, he seemed solicitous of her welfare. But it was the sort of solicitude he might have displayed toward some rather distant relation. Sometimes Laura wondered how it was that they had produced two sons.

Red-haired Jenny, the other newly hired maid, brought them mock turtle soup. When the girl had gone, Laura asked, "Those portraits along the upstairs corridor. Are they all Calvertons?"

"Yes. Calvertons and the women they married. I'll show them to you tomorrow morning. And perhaps after that you'd like to go horseback riding. You do ride, don't you?"

"A little." At two of the Long Island farms that had offered Benjamin Harmon and his wife and daughter hospitality each year, there had been saddle horses. "But it has been years since I have ridden, and I have no riding habit."

"There is an old one of mine here. I think it will fit you. I used to be slimmer. And Zach will select a gentle horse for you."

Throughout the rest of the meal—cold sliced chicken and steamed asparagus and raspberry ice—Lady Parrington talked of the days ahead of them at Walmsley. Most of her talk centered on her granddaughter, of course—how much Lily was going to enjoy petting the spring lambs, and looking for wild strawberries, and visiting the dovecotes.

Laura went upstairs before ten o'clock. Without lighting a lamp, she went to her window and looked out. A three-quarter moon rode in the deep blue sky, its light bright enough that she could make out the distant church steeple. On the hills nearer by, white shapes moved slowly. For a second or two she wondered what they were. Then her ear caught the music of sheep bells.

After breakfast the next morning, Lady Parrington led Laura along that corridor portrait gallery. Calvertons looked back at them from the ornate frames. Dorothy Calverton's father, Howard, at the age of thirty in a high collar and elaborately tied stock of the early eighteen hundreds. Then her grandfather, Henry Calverton, in powdered wig, beruffled shirt, and blue coat with brass buttons.

Laura gave an exclamation. "How very much he looked like Richard!" It was true. Except for the white wig, it might have been her young husband smiling out at her from the gold-leafed frame.

"Yes, Richard looked very much like his

great-grandfather." Lady Parrington's voice held the sadness that always came into it at any mention of her dead son. Too late, Laura wished she had not commented on the resemblance.

They went on. Laura had a sense of moving not only along the gallery but backward in time. Back to another Howard Calverton, who had financed a settlement in the Carolinas. Still farther back to Jeremy Calverton, who had fought for King Charles in the Civil War. And then finally to a beruffed James Calverton who, nearly a hundred years before Walmsley was built, had won Queen Elizabeth's favor by helping thwart an assassination attempt upon her as she and her attendants were out hunting one autumn day. She had rewarded him not only with considerable wealth but with thousands of acres of land that the Crown, during the reign of her father Henry the Eighth, had confiscated from the monasteries. Thus with one stroke she had raised the Calvertons from the status of yeomen to that of landed gentry.

"Well, that's the lot," Lady Parrington said. "Now, shall we hunt up that old riding habit for you?"

Laura thoroughly enjoyed the next few days. She delighted in the entranced look on

Lily's face as, with old Zach grasping the lead rein, the child rode the fat-backed pony around the stable yard. She shared with her daughter the excitement of looking for sweet wild strawberries on the hillsides and the pleasure of petting a lamb's soft wool. Almost equally, Laura enjoyed her solitary hours. Perched sidesaddle on Nell, an aged dapple gray who probably could not have galloped even if pursued by wolves, she rode over the softly rounded hills, across stone-fenced fields where daisies and buttercups and wild geraniums grew among the tall grasses, and through the village of Darcley Wells, where people smiled from open door-ways and sometimes called out greetings as she rode past the white plaster houses with their thatched roofs. Because the newly hired servants had come from this village, she was not surprised to see that they seemed to know who she was.

On her first day's ride she stopped midway of the high street at a chemist's shop. Lady Parrington, who for some mysterious reason suffered a light skin rash each spring, had asked her to buy medication for it. The shop's proprietor, a plump, clean-shaven man named Mr. Proudfoot, had the dignified aplomb of a professional man. Laura did not find that strange. Her mother-in-law had told her that Mr. Proudfoot was the nearest thing to a doctor the village possessed. Laura emerged from the shop and rode on.

About twenty minutes later she reined in atop a hill and looked to the south. Miles away, sunlight glinted on water, and she realized she must be looking at the English Channel. If she had a spyglass, she reflected, she might be able to see the coast of France.

On her second day's ride she guided Nell through the village and then stopped before the church whose distant steeple she had seen from her window. Built from native flintstone that glistened in the sun, it stood in a churchyard filled with gravestones. Although she knew little of church architecture, she judged this church to be not very ancient, not by English standards. Three hundred years old or a little more, perhaps.

A mounting block stood beside the entrance to the gravel path that led up to the church's opened doors. She stepped down onto the block and then secured Nell's reins to a hitching post. As she went up the path an elderly man, evidently a sexton, called out, "Good day, ma'am," and then went on gathering up twigs from the grass and placing them in a cloth bag that hung from one bent shoulder.

She crossed the church porch and went from bright sunlight to dimness. No matter what it had been when founded, apparently this was a "low" church now, because no incense perfumed the air and no candles burned at the altar. The little church had its splendors, though, in the form of tombs, some bearing effigies of the deceased, that were set in the thick walls. As she moved down a side aisle through light filtering through stained glass windows, she saw that they were nearly all tombs of Calvertons. Here was James Calverton, founder of the family fortunes, his carved stone image lying there in Elizabethan ruff and pointed beard, his hands folded on his chest. Beside him was the effigy of his wife in a farthingale and winged cap. Here were James's son and daughter-in-law, Howard and Ann Calverton. The next tombs were those of Howard's three younger brothers and the wives of two of them.

By the early seventeen hundreds, Laura saw, there was no more room in the sidewalls, and so later Calvertons had been laid to rest beneath the church floor, with inscribed slabs marking their graves.

She went out into the sunlight. As she moved down the path, she and the sexton exchanged farewells. Then, perched on Nell's broad back, she rode at a stately pace toward Walmsley.

But if the days were pleasant, the nights were much less so. In London she'd had matters to occupy her mind in the interval between going to bed and falling asleep. She would think about a discussion she'd had with Hugh Malverne on the way home from the League offices, or about whether or not to instruct her pupils in embroidery as well as plain sewing, or about the best way to phrase the League's latest fund-raising letter. But here in this isolated house, with no sound at night except the distant ringing of sheep bells or, beyond the open door of the next room, Lily murmuring something unintelligible in her sleep, Laura found her thoughts reverting again and again to Clive Parrington. Why was he, at the age of thirty-three, still unmarried? Why did he seem so determined not to give rein to the attraction he obviously felt for her? And why, oh why, was he so bent on getting rid of both her and Lily?

Sometimes as she lay there in the darkness he occupied her mind so completely that she almost felt he was not back there in London, doing the lord only knew what, but somewhere beneath the roof of this ancient house.

A little more than a week after her arrival at Walmsley, she rode on Nell toward the hill that afforded a glimpse of the distant Channel. It was a poignantly beautiful morning of sparkling sunlight and of a sky that looked all the more blue because of a few small fleecy clouds drifting across it. Now, at the height of the mating season, the air was clamorous with birdsong. Their voices and the whisper of wind through the long grass and the tinkling of sheep bells blended into a kind of music.

At the crest of the hill she slid from the sidesaddle onto the wide stump of an oak that now, as on other occasions, served her as a mounting block. She tied Nell's reins to a nearby oak sapling that, in another hundred years, might be as huge as its parents must have been before time or weather or the axes of farmers in need of lumber had brought it down.

She sat on the grass, her riding crop beside her, and looked out over the gently rolling hills to that distant patch of sundazzled water. Her thoughts drifted. Had Richard ever visited this hilltop? It seemed likely. She thought of his mother's people, the Calvertons, and of that first Claverton to emerge from obscurity, that yeoman farmer who had foiled an attack on Queen Elizabeth. That led her to thoughts of Phillip of Spain, who had launched his Armada against Elizabeth's England. She had read that the night after wreckage from the Spanish ships, which had been defeated by strong winds and British naval guns, began to wash up on England's beaches, bonfires of celebration had blazed on hilltops from one end of the kingdom to the other. Had a fire burned on this particular hill? Very probably, since this seemed to be the highest ground for a considerable distance.

She was so deep in her thoughts of that deliriously joyful night three hundred years before that Nell's sudden whinny made her jump. She looked over her shoulder and then sprang to her feet. A man was riding up the hill on a big chestnut horse with a white blaze. She recognized the horse as one from the Walmsley stable, a spirited one that old Zach had warned her not to come near. Its rider was Clive Parrington.

Heartbeats rapid, she watched him approach. He slid to the ground and tethered the chestnut to another oak sapling about twenty feet away. Suddenly, she wished she had bothered to take in the too-roomy waist of Lady Parrington's old riding habit and to lengthen its too-short sleeves.

Perhaps the thought communicated itself to him, because when he halted a few feet away from her, the first thing he said was, "That habit doesn't fit you very well, does it?" Then his face flushed, and she knew, with a surge of pleasure, that he must be feeling as tense and awkward as she herself was. Otherwise he would not have chosen that unorthodox greeting.

She said, "It's your mother's. Your step-mother's, I mean." When he didn't answer, she said, "Did you come on the ten-thirty train?" She had heard the distant train whistle as she rode across the fields toward the hilltop.

He nodded.

Why, she wondered, had he come here? Oh, she knew he must have prepared some logical-sounding explanation. But could his real reason be that his thoughts, as he lay in his darkened room in the London house, had kept going to her, just as hers had to him?

She asked, "Did you know I was up here?"

"On Bailey's Hill? I thought you probably

were. Zach said you'd mentioned riding to this place."

His dark eyes regarded her somberly for a moment. Then he said, "I might as well tell you why I'm here." He spoke rapidly, as if eager to get the words out. "My father and I have talked the matter over thoroughly and have decided to make you a proposal."

"A—a proposal?"

"Yes. If you will agree to return to New York, we will deposit fifty thousand dollars to your account in a New York bank. I'm sure that you will consider this arrangement infinitely preferable to an allowance, which you might fear would be cut off. With fifty thousand dollars you can establish just about any sort of life you like for yourself and Lily. If you choose, you can leave it in the bank and live quite comfortably off the interest."

And just a few moments before, she had thought his presence here might mean that he had been irresistibly drawn to her.

Despite the warm sunlight, her face felt cold, and she knew the blood must have drained from it. She searched her mind for words sufficiently cruel to pay him back for the humiliating blow he had dealt her.

"I don't accept bribes, however large." Her voice was thick. "If you and your father want to put his grandchild out into the street, and me along with her, I can't stop you. But I'm not going to make things easy for you by taking your money. Do you understand?"

Not fully aware of what she was doing, she bent and picked up her riding crop. "Do you understand, you—you insulting—" She drew back her arm to strike.

He seized her wrist and gave it a slight twist. She cried out and let go of the riding crop.

"Oh, darling! Did I hurt you that much?" His face had paled. "I don't want to hurt you at all. Oh, Laura! Don't do this to us!"

Feeling the sudden triumphant surge of her blood, she regarded him silently. For several seconds they looked at each other. Then he gave a kind of groan and caught her close to him. She felt the shock of his kiss all through her body. Her arms went around his neck, one hand cupping the back of his dark head.

When he finally lifted his lips from hers, she said, in a shaken voice, "You love me, don't you? *Don't you?*"

He released her, stepped back. "All right." His voice was strangely flat. "I love you. But that doesn't change things. I still want you to go back to New York."

"But why? *Why?*"

"I can't tell you why. Just go! Accept my father's offer. Do it for your own sake and Lily's. In New York you'll be a young and beautiful widow with a small fortune. Surely it won't be long before you meet some man who'll be a good husband to you and a good father to Lily. Now for God's sake, *go.*"

He strode to the tethered chestnut horse. Unaware of the small, triumphant smile on her lips, she watched him mount and ride off toward Walmsley. She kept watching until, rounding the base of a lower hill about a quarter of a mile away, he was lost to her sight.

She sat down then and stared unseeing across the downs to that patch of sun-dazzled water. She felt the same tingling excitement she had known as she slipped out a rear window to meet Richard in the soft Long Island dark. No, not the same. She was older now, and the passion she felt was stronger, hotter, more determined.

Since Clive would not tell her what stood between them, she would find out for herself. One thing was certain. She was not going back to New York, with or without Sir Joseph's bribe. She sat there, making plans.

Finally, with a start, she realized that the sun had moved well past its meridian. Too deep in thought to feel hungry, she had missed her midday meal. Well, no matter. With Lily's grandmother and Cornelia there as well as the servants, she could be sure that Lily had been properly fed.

She got to her feet and untethered old Nell.

Twenty

As SHE RODE toward Walmsley, she again heard a distant steam whistle and knew it must be the two-thirty train for London. Was Clive aboard it? Almost certainly. After that encounter on the hilltop, she could scarcely expect him to join her and the other two women at the dinner table. Well, no matter. As soon as she could manage, she herself would be back in London.

In the stable yard she turned the dapple gray over to Zach and then went through a side entrance to the house and along a corridor to the staircase. When she reached the landing, she noticed that the door to Cornelia Slate's room, a few feet beyond the head of the stairs, stood open. As she started past it

214

she looked in and saw that Cornelia, seated at a small desk, had turned toward the doorway. She called, "Hello," and when Laura paused she added, "You missed luncheon."

"I know. I lost track of the time."

"Clive was here." Cornelia's eyes were bright with malicious curiosity. "He seemed quite upset about something, perhaps even angry."

So apparently, Laura thought, Cornelia had perceived her attraction to Clive. Aloud she said evenly, "He did?"

"Yes. And right after luncheon he left to catch the London train."

"I see." It was obvious, Laura thought, that Cornelia was never going to forgive her for marrying Richard. Or perhaps that wasn't her chief crime in Cornelia's eyes. Perhaps what galled Cornelia most was that she had been provoked into revealing that old dream of hers that she might become Richard's wife.

Laura said, "Do you happen to know if Lily is with her grandmother?"

"No. Lily is in her room. Lady Parrington put her to bed for her nap."

"Well, I'd best go change."

Lady Parrington's room was near the junction of the main corridor with the one leading to the east wing. Laura hesitated at her door and then knocked. Bidden to enter, she opened the door and found her mother-in-law knitting still another pair of small mittens, red ones this time. Laura reflected that by next winter Lily ought to have enough mittens to last her the rest of her childhood.

"Sit down, my dear."

"Thank you, but I must change, and so I'll stay only a moment or two. Mainly I wanted to apologize for having missed luncheon."

"That was quite all right. We didn't worry because Clive told us that he had happened to see you up on Bailey's Hill, and that you seemed perfectly fine." She cast a stitch and then said, "He came up from London with some papers for me to sign. Something about a property a cousin of mine has willed me. And then, because he had two hours until train time, he decided to take a ride."

Laura looked at the older woman's bland face. Did she actually believe that Clive's main objective had been to have some papers signed, or that he had just happened to ride up to Bailey's Hill?

"I see." She started toward the door and then turned back. "Perhaps I'd best tell you right now. I want to go back to London by the end of the week at the latest."

Lady Parrington looked dismayed. "But I thought we would stay here the rest of the month!"

"I know. But I'm really needed at the League. There are never enough volunteers."

"Lily loves this place so! Her pony, the lambs—"

"I know. But you said that the whole family comes down here each August. That's not so far away."

"That's true, but—" She broke off and then said brightly, "I know! Leave Lily here with me the rest of the month."

Because of Lady Parrington's indulgence and flattery, Lily had already developed an excessive fondness for sugarplums and a tendency to gaze admiringly at herself in the mirror. Left for days on end in Grandmother's sole care, she might turn into a very spoiled little girl indeed.

"I'm sorry, but I'm afraid I would miss her too much."

Lady Parrington sighed. "Very well. We'll all go to London."

"Oh! I didn't mean for you to cut short—"

"I wouldn't want to stay here with no one but Cornelia. Besides, I suppose I should also get back to London. I've been planning to have the small drawing room done, and it's better to get the work started now, so that we can be sure it will be completed by fall."

"I suppose that might be best." Laura hesitated, wanting desperately to ask questions about Clive. But no. If she did, Lady Parrington probably would tell her husband or her stepson. And Laura wanted none of the Parringtons to realize how determined she was to learn the truth.

Again, she turned toward the door. "Then I'll see you at dinner."

It was late Sunday afternoon when the hansom cab that had brought them from Waterloo Station deposited them at the tall house in Bostwick Square. The sounds of their arrival apparently had brought Sir Joseph out of his study next to the library, because its door stood open. With Mrs. Mockton and Bessie hovering in the background, Sir Joseph spoke courteously to his daughter-in-law and to Cornelia Slate, kissed his wife's cheek, stroked Lily's pale blond head for a moment, and then returned to his study.

Clive was nowhere visible. But then, Laura had not expected him to be.

Upstairs, she turned her daughter over to

Bessie, who led the excited child up to the nursery to see Fluff. After removing her hat and smoothing her hair, Laura descended to the lower floor and knocked on the study door. Sir Joseph called, "Come in."

Seated behind a flat-topped desk, he got to his feet at her entrance. From the look on his face she gathered that her visit was not unexpected.

"Sit down, my dear." Then, when they were seated facing each other across the desk, "Was your train journey pleasant?"

"Yes," she said, and then went straight to the point. "As I'm sure you know, your son came down to Walmsley a few days ago."

He nodded, his eyes wary.

"He said that you would pay me fifty thousand dollars if my daughter and I returned to New York. I declined the offer."

"So Clive told me." From a certain expectant shine in the deep-set eyes she knew he was hoping that she had changed her mind.

"I can't possibly accept such a proposal. But on the other hand, I can scarcely remain beneath your roof when you have made your eagerness to be rid of me so plain. And so my daughter and I will leave as soon as possible."

"Leave? And go where?"

"Somewhere in London. Edith Riffton and I have become good friends. I am sure she will help me find gainful employment, and if necessary help me out with a loan."

Consternation in Sir Joseph's face. "No! Don't do that." He broke off for a moment. Then he said, with a fumbling ineptitude that she knew must be very rare for him, "It's not that we want to be—rid of you. We've grown fond of both you and Lily. But from the beginning we've feared that your presence would revive—talk about a very painful period in our lives. I refer to our troubles with—Richard." He seemed to find it hard even to speak his dead son's name.

Despite a twinge of sympathy for him, she said, "And then I went to see Belle Mulroney. That is what finally decided you to make an offer you felt I would find irresistible."

He nodded.

"Is it so utterly unheard of, Sir Joseph, a connection between a rich man's son and a lower-class young woman? It's called sowing wild oats, isn't it? And the result, as in Belle's case, is sometimes an illegitimate child. Why were you so upset by my finding out about it?"

Obviously disconcerted by her frankness,

he said awkwardly, "I know I must seem very out of fashion. In my day ladies were protected against even knowing about— Perhaps I'll never grow used to— What are they called, the ladies like Mrs. Besant and Edith Riffton? The New Women?"

Again he broke off and then said, "But if you are going to remain in London, we would much, much prefer that you go on living here. People would think it strange indeed if our daughter-in-law and her child lived in cheap lodgings somewhere."

Was that his real reason, fear of embarrassment in the Parringtons' social circle? Perhaps. But as far as Laura could see, Sir Joseph had no social life beyond his club, and Lady Parrington had not even that. True, twice a month, in the Parrington carriage, she ventured out to pay calls, but that was a procedure that seemed to consist mainly of leaving her card at various houses. In return, other women left their cards on a silver tray, tendered by Mrs. Mockton, at the Parrington house, although now and then a beplumed and bejeweled caller had swept up the stairs to spend twenty minutes with Lady Parrington in her sitting room. About the only visitor she had received frequently, at least during Laura's stay there, had been her young neighbor, Valerie Lockwood.

No, Laura was sure Sir Joseph had a much stronger reason for feeling that if she were to remain in London it would be best that she go on living beneath his roof. That way it would be much easier for him to keep track of her movements and to be aware of anything that she might discover.

"Please stay," Sir Joseph said.

Again she felt a surge of sympathy for this able, rich, and yet obviously anxiety-ridden man. But it did not lessen her determination to find out what stood between herself and Clive Parrington, and why he and his father had turned so completely against the flawed but nevertheless loving and charming man who had been her husband.

"Lily and I will stay. And thank you. Thank you very much."

He inclined his head.

"Just one thing more," Laura said. "Does Lady Parrington know about the offer you made to me?"

"No, not unless you yourself told her. Did you?"

"No. There seemed to be no reason to, since I had no intention of accepting the offer. Besides, I didn't like to upset her.

And she would be very upset indeed if she knew you had tried to separate her granddaughter from her." She paused. "Did you and your son take that into account when you decided upon that proposal to me? Didn't you realize how distressed she would be if I had accepted your offer and taken Lily back to America?"

"We did." His tone and his expression had hardened. For a moment she caught a glimpse of the steely will that had enabled him to climb from a clerk's job to wealth and a knighthood. "My wife would just have had to accept the situation, that's all."

So much for her former belief that Lady Parrington's wishes would prevail, if and when it came to a question of whether or not her granddaughter would be separated from her. Laura said, "I'll say good-bye for now. I must go upstairs and unpack."

She realized that there was little chance that Clive would be present at dinner. After all, even before their encounter on Bailey's Hill, he frequently had stayed away from the family table. Nevertheless, she came to the dining room that night tense with the hope of seeing him.

He was not there. And less than three hours later she learned from Bessie that there was little chance he would be in the future. Bessie said, wielding the hairbrush, "I guess you know that Mr. Clive has moved away."

"Away!"

"Yesterday he had Mrs. Mockton pack most of his clothes and send them to his club."

Bessie could not help feeling a bit of satisfaction over the dismay that had leaped into Mrs. Richard's mirrored face. Bessie knew that Mr. Clive had gone down to Walmsley. She had heard it from Martha, who had heard it from Mrs. Mockton, who had overheard Sir Joseph and Mr. Clive talking about train schedules. Bessie had hoped that there in the country, what with the spring flowers and the birds and all, Mrs. Richard would bring him to the point of proposing. But she must have made a fine mess of everything, because now he wasn't even going to live at home anymore.

It really didn't matter, Laura was telling herself, that they would no longer be sleeping beneath the same roof. For a moment there she had feared he had gone abroad someplace. But he was still in London. That was the important thing.

The next afternoon at the League offices, Edith Riffton greeted Laura with open arms and with loads of accumulated work. It was past four when Laura was free to descend the stairs and turn right along a street that, after those days in the spring-bright countryside, looked uglier and dirtier than ever. She turned left onto Bengali Street. As before, the door beneath Billy Barker's sign stood open. Not even glancing into the establishment's main room, she went down the narrow hall, climbed the creaking stairs, and knocked on the door just beyond the landing.

There was no sound of movement behind the thin, scarred panels. She knocked again, waited.

"Belle ain't there."

The voice had come from the hall below. Laura looked over the railing into Billy Barker's fat, upturned face. "Where is she?"

He shrugged. "Who knows?"

Quickly she descended the stairs. "Surely you must have some idea."

"All I know is, she and her kid went off with a cove named Jim Jones. Merchant sailor, he is, from Bristol or Liverpool. Or maybe Newcastle."

Laura said, dismayed, "Didn't she leave an address?"

"Not her! And now I see why. She borrowed money from me just before she left. Said she'd send it back to me right away. That was ten days ago."

He peered at her downcast face. Although it seemed to him most unlikely, he asked, "Does Belle owe you money, too?"

"Oh, no. It's just that I wanted to ask her—" She broke off and then said, "I needed to talk to her about—Coleen's father. That is her daughter's name, isn't it?"

"That's right. Coleen."

"Did you know her father?"

"Know him? I never even knew who he was. Belle's always had a lot of admirers." He grinned. "And she's been generous with them, if you take my meaning."

For a moment Laura was silent. It had suddenly struck her as odd that within days of her interview with Belle, the woman had gone off with some man. Was it possible that the man had been paid to persuade her to do just that?

"This man Belle left with, this Smith—"

"Jones. Jim Jones."

"Had Belle known him long?"

"For years. He always turned up here between voyages and tried to get her to quit the music hall. Jealous, the poor fool, afraid of what she was up to while he was at sea.

Well, he finally got her." He added indignantly, "And the ten quid she borrowed from me along with her."

Laura reflected that her suspicions were probably groundless. If Belle had known her sailor friend for years, it was probably only a coincidence that she had finally agreed at this particular time to go away with him.

Was Belle in one of those ports her former employer had mentioned? Probably. But which one? And even if she knew which one, how could she, with almost no funds, track down a man with as common a name as Jones in a city of a hundred thousand or more?

She told herself grimly that she would just have to think of some other way of tackling the problem.

"Well, if you do hear from her, will you let me know? You can send me a message at the League offices."

"I'll do that, ma'am. What was your name again?"

"Mrs. Parrington, Laura Parrington. I'll write it down for you."

Reaching into her reticule, she brought out a small notebook and a pencil, wrote briefly, and ripped out the page. "Here you are. And thank you."

Aware of his following gaze, she walked down the corridor and out onto the sidewalk. A vaguely familiar-looking man in a brown suit and brown bowler hat stood in a doorway directly across the street. After a moment she realized where she had seen him before. He had been standing across from the League offices when she descended the stairs to the street.

Another coincidence? Possibly. But it seemed to her far more likely that Sir Joseph was keeping an eye on her.

Well, let him.

She walked toward Tower Bridge and the omnibus that, drawn by its team of draft horses, would take her within a few yards of Bostwick Square.

Twenty-One

LAURA'S FAINT HOPE that she might find Clive Parrington at the dinner table was not fulfilled. But Valerie Lockwood was there, more animated than ever. She flirted discreetly with Sir Joseph and listened with flattering attentiveness to Lady Parrington's account of a Buckingham Palace ball she had attended the year before her marriage. As she watched the Parringtons' lovely young neighbor, Laura felt an uneasiness that, after a moment, she had to recognize as jealousy. True, Valerie made no mention of seeing Clive. But her manner toward Laura was friendlier than before, as if she were ceasing to regard her as a rival. To her dismay, Laura realized that the hand with which she held her fork was a little unsteady.

The next evening in the League workroom, as she moved about among her needlework pupils, praising a neat flat fell seam, or recommending that a darn with a ragged edge be done over, she kept hoping in vain that some urchin would appear with a note from Billy Barker about Belle. Later on, as a cab holding her and Hugh Malverne moved toward Bostwick Square, she was quiet and abstracted for much of the way. Then, realizing that the young doctor had subsided into hurt silence, she roused herself enough to describe the beauties of Walmsley and to talk about her class that night and to ask him about his work at the clinic. By the time he said good night to her just outside the door of the Parrington house, his smile was warm. As she looked up into the pleasant face with the neat blond beard, she found herself almost wishing that she had never encountered Clive Parrington. If she had not, by now she might be looking forward confidently and happily to Hugh Malverne's marriage proposal.

Three days passed. Still she received no word from the music hall manager. Reluctantly, she concluded that in all probability Belle was lost to her as a source of information.

On Friday when she left the League offices, she turned not toward Tower Bridge but toward Bengali Street. She would try to find out if Billy Barker knew anything about that dreadful old woman who had called to her from outside the little park's gate that early spring day. She did not find the project a pleasant one. She didn't even like to remember that scarecrow creature who in a drunken, roundabout fashion had seemed to be claiming some knowledge of Richard. But perhaps her claim was true. Perhaps she really could tell Laura things that she very much needed to know.

She turned in under the music hall's sign. Billy Barker was in the establishment's main room. He stood on the stage, watching a thin man of at least seventy who was touching up the backdrop's Venetian scene. At the moment he was daubing black paint onto the gondola.

"Mr. Barker?"

The fat man turned around. He said in a genial tone, "So it's you again, ma'am."

"May I talk to you for a moment?"

"That you may." He turned to the painter. "Better put a second coat on that balcony. The cracks still show." He came down the steps. "This way," he said, and led her back to the table and chair where he had been sitting the first time she saw him. Evidently he regarded this part of the big room as his office. He pulled a second straight chair out from the wall and with a flourish of his hand indicated that she was to sit.

When they were both seated, Laura said, "You haven't heard from Belle Mulroney?"

"That I haven't. Not a word, not a shilling."

"Mr. Barker, didn't you tell me that you had lived in the East End a long time?"

"All my life. Sixty-three years."

"Then you must know a lot of people."

He cocked his head to one side. "Just who are you talking about, Mrs. Parrington?"

"I don't know her name. She just appeared one day outside the little park in Bostwick Square. I was sitting on a bench

231

inside. She called to me. She knew my name, or at least my husband's. She called me Mrs. Richard Parrington."

"Didn't you ask her who she was?"

"Yes, but she was quite drunk. All she really told me, before this policeman came along and chased her away, was that she was somebody's mother, somebody she referred to only as 'her.' "

Should she tell him about the attack upon her as she sat in the fog-shrouded park the next day? No, she decided. If he thought that a crime were involved, he might refuse to continue the conversation.

"Then sometime later, someone—gave me some information about Belle Mulroney, and I got the notion that *she* might be the daughter this old woman was talking about. But Belle told me that both her parents are dead, back in Ireland."

"And so they are. What did she look like, this woman who came up to you in the square?"

"Quite dreadful. Dirty and ragged and with an old straw hat ornamented with cloth roses. The odd part was that she was wearing black lace mitts." Again she saw the gnarled and dirty hands, clad in elegant lace to the knuckles, reaching through the bars.

Aggie, Billy Barker thought. Aggie Thompson. It was the lace mitts that cinched it. About twenty years before, wandering around someplace in the West End—that was a bad habit of Aggie's, going into neighborhoods where she didn't belong—she had found a pair of black lace mitts on the sidewalk, still in their store wrapping. They had delighted her so much that, when they wore out, she had managed to acquire a new pair. Since she never seemed to be without lace mitts, lord knew how many pairs she had worn out over the years.

Poor Aggie. Not many people today would believe what she had looked like fifty-odd years ago, when she had been the star attraction at Captain Kidd's, a music hall in Limehouse. Not that she was much of a singer. Truth was, she had a voice like a crow's. But when she stood up there on the stage with plumes in her hair—flaming red, it was—and a spangled costume that left her plump shoulders bare and ended just below the knees of her silk-stocking legs, nobody cared how she sounded.

Even though he'd been still a nipper then, he'd been daft about Aggie. One whole summer he'd hung around Captain Kidd's, hoping Aggie would smile at him, or rumple his hair, or give him an errand to run. Come to think of it, maybe it was because of memories of her that he'd decided, later on, to go into the music hall business. And now Aggie, done in by drink and her troubles and the years, was the nearest thing to a living scarecrow you'd want to see.

But Billy still had a soft spot in his heart for her. That was why he had no intention of telling the young American woman anything definite until he could be sure it would bring Aggie no harm.

"Maybe I do know somebody like that. But why would you be wanting to find her, ma'am?"

So, Laura realized, this man could help her. But obviously he didn't intend to until she had confided in him a little more. "I—I need to know a few things about my late husband. You see, before I met him his family had—had persuaded him to go to America and stay there."

That was the rich for you, Billy thought. If they had a son they thought was a family disgrace, they'd ship him off to India or America or someplace. One thing you could say for the poor. They might knock their kids about, but they didn't disown them.

Laura went on, "Until I came here I

thought it was because he couldn't seem to stop gambling that his family had finally turned him out, but now I think there may have been—something more."

"Seems to me Belle could have told you a lot about him. I mean—well, meaning no offense, ma'am, but the last time you was here you asked if I knew who was the father of Belle's kid. That gave me the feeling that your husband was, and that you knew it."

"Yes, I knew it." Best to be frank with him, she had decided, at least up to a point. "And I think Belle *could* have told me some things." Laura did not know whether the Irishwoman's reticence sprang from kind-heartedness or from some other motive, but she'd had a distinct impression that Belle was withholding information.

"You think she was keeping things back, eh?"

"Yes."

For Billy that put a different light on the matter. He had a grudge against Belle, first for walking out on her job, and second for not sending him the ten quid she'd bor-rowed. If she'd tried to keep this Mrs. Parrington from finding out something, then maybe he could even the score by helping her to do so.

He said, "This old woman, the one with the lace mitts. You wouldn't be planning to make trouble for her, would you?"

"Oh, no! I just want to talk to her. I have nothing against her."

Unless, of course, she had been the one who had entered the park that fog-shrouded afternoon, some sort of weapon in her hand. But Laura felt that was highly unlikely. In the first place the old woman, no matter how drunken or corrupt, had not conveyed an impression of violence. In the second place it seemed improbable that she would have returned to the park the very day after a policeman had threatened to take her "in charge."

Billy Barker still seemed undecided. Laura reached into her reticule. "If you could tell me where I could find the woman, I'll try to make it worth your while." As she laid a five-pound note on the table, she tried not to dwell on the thought that now she had less than twenty pounds left to her name.

Billy looked at the banknote. That settled it. Here was a way to get back half the ten quid Belle had bilked him out of. He said, pocketing the note, "Her name is Aggie Thompson, and she's had a hard life." Maybe no more so than some others, he added mentally, but still hard. "I hope I'm doing the right thing."

"You are. As I told you, I have no intention of making trouble for her. Now please tell me where I can find her."

"I couldn't say where she sleeps. Lots of places, probably. If I had to make a guess, I'd say most nights she's in Battle Lane, in that row of old stables they call the workhouse annex. But I know you wouldn't want to look there."

"Then where—"

"I hear she spends a few hours most days at The Blue Boar near Billingsgate Wharf. An omnibus will take you within a hundred yards of it."

She thanked him and left. Out on the sidewalk she saw no sign of the man in the brown suit. But ten minutes later, as she was nearing Tower Bridge, she looked back over her shoulder and there he was.

Twenty-Two

BY THE TIME the omnibus left her near the Parrington house, she was aware of a rawness in her throat and a slight ache throughout her body. A cold coming on, she thought.

One of her pupils a few nights earlier had been sniffling and sneezing.

As soon as she had finished her dinner she said good night to the Parringtons and went up to her room. When she awoke the next morning, she felt even more wretched. She let Lily dress herself. When Bessie came to take the child up to the nursery for breakfast, Laura asked that her own breakfast be brought to her room. "And will you please ask Mrs. Mockton to phone Mrs. Riffton at the League office? I won't be able to come there tonight. I'd appreciate it if she'd call Dr. Malverne with the same message."

She stayed in bed for three days. Mrs. Mockton installed a small spirit stove in her room so that if she were asleep when her meals arrived, they could be kept warm for her.

When she did finally get up, still feeling weak, she took an omnibus not to the League offices but to the East End dock area known as Billingsgate. The street she walked down was just as dirty as the one on which the League's office building stood, but there was a certain vitality here that the Spitalfield area lacked. Perhaps it was because the fishing industry provided employment for most of the neighborhood's inhabitants. Perhaps it was the whistles of barges and fishing vessels as they neared the wharf. Perhaps it was the voices of men and women calling to each other along the sidewalk, or up to people leaning out of tenement windows, or from one heavily laden cart to another. As if determined to live up to the area's reputation for coarse invective, they shouted obscene insults, sometimes jovially and sometimes apparently with real rancor. Even children playing in the gutter used words that, until she had joined Edith Riffton's forces, Laura had never heard.

And the air was redolent of fish, so much so that when she reached the doorway of The Blue Boar, she almost welcomed the fumes of ale and gin and tobacco. As she hesitated on the threshold of the crowded but suddenly silent room, a burly man of about forty-five hurried forward. He wore a long, far-from-clean white apron. "What can I do for you, ma'am?"

"I'm looking for a Mrs. Aggie Thompson." Laura had no idea whether or not the old woman had ever married, but it seemed tactful to grant her the title of Mrs.

"Aggie? I'll take you to her, ma'am. She's the one alone over there in the corner."

"Thank you," Laura said hastily, "but there's no need to take me to her. I see her."

Baffled curiosity in his face, the man stepped back. As she threaded her way through tables filled with silent, avid-eyed men and women, she realized how strange she must look in this place, a young woman in mourning clothes.

"Mrs. Thompson? Mrs. Aggie Thompson?"

Aggie, who had been staring into the depths of her cup of gin, raised blurred-looking eyes to Laura's face. She said after several seconds, "Who the hell are you?"

"Don't you remember me? You came to the park in Bostwick Square, and you called me by name. I'm Laura Parrington, Richard Parrington's widow."

Recognition came into the old face. Mitted hand tightening around her cup, she shrank back in her chair. "I didn't do you no harm!"

"I didn't say you did. It's just that—"

"I'm not the one who bashed you the next day!"

After a moment Laura asked, "But you knew about it?"

"Only because it was in the papers! I never took up with reading, but this friend of mine, a bloke who used to work on the wharf, he can read. He reads the police reports in the paper every day, and sometimes he tells me about them. He said that someone had knocked the daughter-in-law of some toff named Sir Joseph Parrington in the head. Of course, I didn't let on."

"Let on?"

"That I knew anything about any Parringtons. I'm paid to keep my mouth about you people, and I do."

"Do you mind if I sit down?"

"You sure you didn't come to make trouble for me?" Her voice became a whine. "I've had enough troubles in my life. Lord knows I have."

"I just want to ask you a few questions. You don't have to answer them if you don't want to."

Curiosity and caution warred in the seamed face. Curiosity won. "All right. Keep your voice down."

After Laura had sat down in one of the vacant chairs at the table, the old woman looked around. A man and a woman, both thin to the point of emaciation, sat at a table a few feet away. Gazing into each other's eyes, they obviously hoped to give the impression of not listening, but Aggie was not fooled.

"Bug off!" she said. "Take your big ears somewhere else."

The woman bristled, but the man said, "All right, Aggie, all right. Don't get yourself in an uproar." They carried their beer mugs to a table about fifteen feet farther away.

The man in the soiled apron was threading his way through the tables. Aggie said, "Hop it, Ben. She don't want to drink anything here, a lady like her." When Ben had walked away, she said to Laura, "All right, dearie. What is it?"

"That day in the park you said that you were being paid a pound a month. The Parringtons are paying it, aren't they?"

A fleeting look in Aggie's eyes confirmed that, although she said nothing aloud.

"Why are they paying you?"

After a moment Aggie said, "Come off it, luv. You know."

"But I don't! If I did I wouldn't be here."

"You were married to him, and still you don't know?"

"No! As I said, I wouldn't be here if—"

"Comes to that, how'd you get here? Who told you where to find me?"

"A man in Spitalfields named Billy Barker." She added hastily, "But he wouldn't

242

tell me until I'd convinced him I meant you no harm."

Billy Barker. To Aggie he still seemed that nipper hanging around Captain Kidd's, his eyes big as saucers while he waited for her to toss him a word or a smile. He'd always been good to her, Billy had. And maybe right now, she thought, with a plan unfolding in her mind, he'd done her the biggest favor of all.

Years and years ago, a man whose name she had forgotten had taken her to Brighton for two days. She'd remembered every moment of it. The salt-water taffy. The amusement pier. The music halls that were ever so much jollier and newer-looking than the ones in Limehouse and Spitalfields and Billingsgate.

When she'd made her arrangement with Sir Joseph Parrington, it had crossed her mind that maybe now she could go live in Brighton. But right away she realized she couldn't, not on a pound a month, not when she needed so much of it for gin. True, she had thought of trying to get more out of him. But he had warned her what would happen to her if she did, and she had taken the warning to heart. The Sir Josephs of the world ran everything, and only fools tried to push them too far.

But now here, perhaps, was a chance to get a lot of money all at once. Two hundred pounds, say. With that much she could buy some new clothes and a train ticket to Brighton. She'd rent lodgings under another name. In her new clothes she'd be able to walk on the amusement pier or anywhere else without the police chasing her away.

And if Sir Joseph sent people looking for her? Well, they'd never think she'd gone to a place like Brighton. And even if they did, they'd have trouble finding her, with her new name and her new clothes, and her respectable lodgings. What's more, she wouldn't drink in pubs, not even the most proper ones. Instead she would buy her gin by the bottle and drink it in her lodgings.

She'd have to give up her black lace mitts, though. Some nark might be able to trace her by them, since everybody in the East End knew that Aggie Thompson always wore lace mitts. Well, that would be a small loss compared to all the other things she'd have.

She said, "All right, dearie. I'll tell you. But it will cost you."

Laura laid her reticule on the table and loosened its drawstring. She tried not to think of how little she would have left if she gave Aggie five pounds.

Aggie said, "I want two hundred quid."

Laura said, aghast, "I don't have that much. I don't have nearly that much."

"Maybe not. But you can get it. You live in a rich house with rich people, don't you?"

"They've never given me anything, not in money."

"Just the same, you can get it one way or another, if you want to bad enough. And I think you do. You want to know something your husband didn't tell you and your in-laws won't tell you. Well, I'll tell you, if you pay me enough.

"You'd better work fast, though." Her voice became sly. "I might decide any day now to move away someplace. Or I might just pop off, an old one like me. Then where'd you be? You'd maybe *never* find out what you need to know. But if you work fast, you'll probably find me right here at this table when you come back with that two hundred quid."

Laura sat rigid, clutching her reticule with both hands. How could she get two hundred pounds? She didn't even have any jewelry or other valuables. She'd sold those belongings to buy her passage and Lily's to England.

Suddenly she realized there was someone who almost certainly would loan her the money.

She said, pushing back her chair, "Very well. I'll bring it to you as soon as I can."

Twenty-Three

BY THE TIME she reached Harley Street, late afternoon shadows had begun to fill Hugh Malverne's waiting room. Only one patient, an elderly woman, sat there among the brown plush sofa and armchairs and copies of *Punch* and *The Tatler*. The inner door opened. Dr. Malverne, ushering out a military-looking man with a gray moustache, gave Laura a surprised smile and then said to the older woman, "Please come in, Lady Warren."

Too tense even to try to read a magazine, Laura sat there for about twenty minutes. Then the elderly woman emerged, and Laura went into the inner office.

When they were seated facing each other across his desk, he asked, "Are you over your cold?"

"Yes. I'm fine now."

"You don't look fine." He studied the pale, taut face.

"It's just that I haven't been sleeping too well, and then something has happened— oh, Hugh! Could you loan me two hundred pounds?"

He said, after a stunned moment, "My dear girl, of course. But what is it? Are you in some sort of difficulty?"

She knew that even if she declined to answer any questions he would still loan her the money. But it would be grossly unfair, she felt, to presume that much on his fondness of her. Surely she owed him at least some explanation.

"There's something I need to know," she said, "something that the Parringtons won't tell me. I guess you know that they—they forced my husband to go to America because he couldn't seem to stop gambling, although of course he wasn't my husband then. Even when I first knew him, I felt that there was more to the story than that."

She went on, telling of the times when Richard, otherwise the most considerate of husbands, withdrew money from their savings without consulting her, money he never replaced. She spoke of Richard's sudden death and of her discovery that she was almost penniless and of her decision, finally, to appeal to her child's English grandparents.

"They were both cold to me when I reached London. For several days they avoided even seeing Lily. But I was sure that once they did, their attitude would change. As it turned out, I was right about that, but in the meantime—" She broke off.

"In the meantime?"

"Other things had happened. That dreadful old woman calling to me through the park gate, and then, the next day, someone striking me down."

"And you felt that all this had something to do with Richard?"

"Yes! The Parringtons and even the police said that this woman must be just—some derelict. But I couldn't believe that."

Again she broke off and then said, "Thanks to you, I went to work for the League. Soon after that I—I learned that before he left England, Richard had had a mistress."

She told him about Belle Mulroney and Billy Barker and, finally, her conversation with Aggie Thompson earlier that afternoon.

"Sir Joseph has been paying her a pound a month for years and years now! I need to know what it is he doesn't want her to tell. And if I pay her two hundred pounds—"

"She'll tell you." He looked at her with troubled eyes. "But doesn't it occur to you that you might be better off *not* knowing what Sir Joseph wants to hide?"

"No! I have a right to know. Richard was my little girl's father. I have a right to know everything about him."

And there was another reason, a compelling one that kept her awake at night. She needed to know what it was that stood between her and Clive Parrington.

But that was one thing she could not tell Hugh. Oh, not out of any fear that he would withhold the money. She knew he would keep his word to loan it to her. But she could not bear the thought of the pain that would come into his pleasant young face if he knew that she was that much in love with another man. Even though she knew that she was being cowardly, she could not bring herself to tell him.

"All right," he said. "I don't have two hundred pounds here in the office. But I'll give you a bank draft that you can cash tomorrow morning."

He reached into the drawer of his desk, brought out a checkbook, and wrote. She accepted the check, so grateful and so embarrassed that all she could do was move her lips in a silent, "Thank you."

"Laura, I think your nervous strain, plus the cold you had, has been too much for you. I want you to go to bed as soon as you reach home."

"I can't."

"Can't?"

"It's Sir Joseph's birthday. There will be a small dinner party tonight. The family plus Valerie Lockwood, who lives two doors away."

Hugh nodded.

"And then there'll be a Brigadier Somebody-or-other and his wife, who are old friends of the Parringtons. And I think one other couple."

She wondered with a leap of her pulse if Clive would be there. Probably. It would look strange indeed if he did not attend his father's birthday dinner.

Hugh frowned. "Well, if you feel you must be at the party. But excuse yourself as early as possible. I'm going to give you something to help you sleep."

He went to his glass-doored medicine cabinet, took out a bottle, and shook several tablets into a small white envelope. "Take one of these just before you go to bed."

She thanked him again, feeling both grateful and guilty, and then went out into the bronze-tinged sunlight of late afternoon.

By the time she reached the Parrington house, reaction had set in. As she climbed the front steps, her tiredness was like leaden weights tied to her ankles. With dismay she realized that she had best follow Hugh's advice, after all, and not go to the dinner party.

In the lower hall she learned that Justin had already arrived. As she passed the library's partially open door, she heard his voice and his father's.

She climbed the stairs to the next floor. Because no one as yet had turned on the gas jets, the hall was shadowy. She had walked several feet along it before she saw, with a leap of her pulse, that Clive had emerged from his room and was moving toward her, his face dark above his white ruffled evening shirt. He stopped.

"Hello, Laura." His voice sounded constrained.

"Hello. So you'll be at your father's birthday dinner."

"I could scarcely miss it, could it?"

"I'm afraid I'll have to. I feel utterly done in."

Even in the dim light she could tell that he felt both relieved and disappointed that they would not be facing each other across the dinner table.

"Have you made your excuses yet?"

"No."

"Shall I make them for you? I was just about to go to my stepmother's room."

"Thank you. I would appreciate it." How civilized we sound, she thought. One would never think that only a few days ago, up on Bailey's Hill—

"Good-bye," she said, and walked on toward the stairs leading to the servants' floor. Up there the hall, with no heavy curtains or draperies hanging at its front or rear windows, was flooded with near-sunset light. She went into the nursery. Bessie and Lily sat at the table eating poached whitefish and green peas, with tea for Bessie and milk for Lily.

"No, no, darling," Laura said as the child ran to her. "I don't want to kiss you until I'm quite sure my cold is over." Hand on her daughter's head, she went on, "Bessie, I'm afraid I can't go to the dinner party tonight. Instead I'm going to bed."

"I'm sorry that you'll miss it, ma'am. But you do look done in."

"Do you think you could bring me a tray?"

"Of course, ma'am. But could it be early like? I'm to help Martha in the dining room tonight."

"Whatever is convenient for you."

"About seven-thirty, say? And I'll bring your cocoa and Lily's about an hour after that. If you don't want it right away, it'll keep warm on that little spirit stove Mrs. Mockton put in your room."

"Thank you very much, Bessie. Please bring Lily down when she's finished her supper."

Even though she made a few ritual protests, Lily consented to go to bed soon after Laura had finished her own dinner. Laura was beside the child's bed, reading aloud from Stevenson's book of verse, when she heard Bessie come into the next room to take away the dinner tray and to leave the cocoa mugs on the spirit stove.

Bessie called a good night, and Laura answered. When she finished the poem she had been reading, she brought Lily's cocoa to her. Then, feeling lightheaded with fatigue, she returned to her own room. She undressed and drank the mug of warm, sweet liquid. Too tired to brush her hair, she swallowed one of the tablets Hugh Malverne had given her, turned out the gas jet, and got into bed.

For a while she lay awake, thinking of Bailey's Hill. She thought, too, of the dinner party downstairs and wondered what Valerie Lockwood was wearing and whether Clive was admiring her. Finally, though, her exhaustion and the effects of the pill overwhelmed her, and she slept.

"Mama!"

The cry, thin and terrified, brought Laura up through layers of sleep. She flung back the bedclothes. Not bothering to cross the room to the gas jet, she groped on the bedside table for matches, lit the oil lamp, and hurried with it into the adjoining room. In its glow Lily's face looked terribly altered, the skin pale and shiny with sweat, her pupils so dilated that her blue eyes looked almost black. Both small fists were pressing into her abdomen.

As Laura set down the lamp on the nightstand, Lily said, "Mama, it hurts," and made a retching sound.

Laura flew across the room, took the basin from the washstand, and set it on the floor beside the bed. "Lean over, Lily. Try to vomit, darling. Try!"

The child again retched, but that was all.

Laura thought, Ipecac! In New York, two months before Richard's death, Laura discovered that Lily had consumed nearly a whole bottle of sweet-tasting cough remedy. The hastily summoned doctor had induced vomiting with a teaspoon full of ipecac and had recommended that Laura keep the emetic on hand. She still had some. Cleaning out the medicine chest before she left New York, she had placed an unopened bottle in her valise. She ran into her room and, by the refracted glow from the oil lamp, hauled her valise down from the wardrobe shelf.

With the bottle in her hand, she thought frantically. A spoon, I need a spoon! Then she remembered her cocoa mug, with the spoon on its accompanying saucer. She hurried to her bedside stand, then carried both the bottle and the spoon back to Lily's room. Her breathing ragged, the child was moaning now.

Willing her hand not to shake, Laura poured out a spoonful of the dark liquid. "Take this, darling. It will make you much better. I promise you."

Lily swallowed the emetic. If Laura remembered correctly, it took a few minutes for the ipecac to work. She returned to her own room, pulled the bellrope beside the fireplace, and lit a gas jet. She put a wrapper of flower-printed cotton over her nightdress. Back in Lily's room, she lit the gas jet beside the bed.

A splattering sound behind her. Thank God, she thought, and turned to see Lily leaning over the basin. Laura sat down on the edge of the bed and held the child's forehead. "Again, darling! Get up more of it if you can. That's my good girl. Now try once more."

At last Lily lay back on the pillow. She looked exhausted, but she was no longer moaning. With a handkerchief from the pocket of her wrapper, Laura wiped the child's mouth. "I'll only be a second, darling." She lifted the basin and went out into the hall.

Mrs. Mockton was hurrying toward her. Laura saw that the housekeeper was still fully dressed. That must mean it was still quite early.

Mrs. Mockton said, "You rang, Mrs. Richard?" Then, looking at the basin, "What happened?"

"My little girl had a stomach upset, a bad one."

"Oh, the poor child! Here, let me—"

"No, no. I can put it down the w.c. What I'd like you to do is to telephone Dr. Malverne at his flat, right away. I think she is all right, but I want to be sure."

"Of course, Mrs. Richard."

In the w.c. Laura emptied the basin, then lifted it to the washstand and turned on both taps. When it was thoroughly washed, she carried it back to Lily's room and placed it on the stand beside its matching pitcher. Then she hurried to the child's bedside. How pale she still was. A knock. Laura said, "Come in."

It was Bessie, looking unfamiliar in the formal black uniform and white apron and cap she had worn to serve at the birthday party. Her normally florid face was so pale that her freckles stood out. "Mrs. Mockton says Miss Lily is sick! She's telephoned for the doctor!"

"I think she's all right now, but—" She broke off and then said distractedly, "I must get dressed before he gets here."

"I'll help you, ma'am."

"No, no. Just sit with Lily."

Laura went back into her room and donned

clothing. She was sitting at her dressing table, thrusting pins into her hair, when she became aware that Bessie stood behind her. "Can't I help you with your hair, ma'am?"

"No, thanks. This will just have to do."

"Very well, ma'am." She went back into the other room.

Twenty-Four

A MOMENT LATER someone knocked. Laura sped across the room and opened the door. "Oh, thank you, thank you, for coming so soon!"

As Hugh Malverne stepped into the room, black leather satchel in hand, she heard a number of voices in the lower hall. Probably some of the dinner guests were leaving. Laura led him into the adjoining room.

Bessie, sitting in the chair beside the bed, sprang to her feet. Laura said, "This is Bessie. She takes care of my daughter."

"Hello, Bessie." While Laura and Bessie looked on, he sat down in the bedside chair and took the child's hand in his own. "Hello, Lily. I'm Dr. Malverne, and I've heard a lot about you. Now tell me what happened."

"I was sick."

"Oh?" His fingers were on the child's pulse.

"My stomach hurt and I wanted to throw up but I couldn't and then Mama gave me some medicine, and I could."

He looked at Laura, who said, "Ipecac. She vomited three times."

He looked back at the child. "My! You *were* sick, weren't you?"

He lifted one of her eyelids, then the other. Taking a stethoscope from the leather bag, he pressed it against the small chest. Finally he removed the instrument's earpieces and said to Laura, "She'll be fine, thanks to the emetic. But her heart action and her dilated pupils definitely suggest some sort of poisoning."

As Laura looked at him, stunned, he said hastily, "Some sort of food poisoning, undoubtedly. But I had best have the material analyzed."

"Material?"

"The material she threw up."

Appalled at her own stupidity, Laura said, "You can't. I took the basin across the hall and emptied it. Then I washed the basin until it was entirely clean. It's over there on the stand."

His gaze followed hers to the china basin.

"Well, it's of no great importance, since she's all right."

"But how could I have been so stupid? I should have realized you'd want to—but I myself wasn't feeling well, and I'd taken that sedative you gave me, and so I just didn't—"

"It's all *right*. Doubtless it was something she had for her supper, something that had turned. After all, today has been quite warm."

Standing at the foot of the bed, Bessie said, "I gave her her supper! It was white-fish and peas, same as I had, with fresh peaches for a sweet. There was nothing wrong with what I gave her!" Her voice was shrill, defensive. "If there was, how is it *I* wasn't—"

"No one's blaming you," Hugh Malverne said. "She may have had some other food she managed to find—"

"She didn't! From breakfast on, she didn't have anything but what I gave her."

He said, turning to the child, "Is that true, Lily? You weren't down in the kitchen today? Or maybe helped yourself from some candy dish?"

Lily shook her head. Bessie said, "The only other thing she had was her cocoa, and Mrs. Richard had that, too."

Hugh Malverne said, his gaze going to Laura, "Cocoa?"

"Yes. Bessie brings a mug for Lily and one for me at bedtime each night."

"Are the mugs still here? There may be some cocoa left in them."

"Yes, they are still here." She looked at the bedside stand and then exclaimed, "Why, Lily's mug *was* here. I saw it there on the stand when I brought in the light and set it down."

"Ma'am?" Bessie's face was suddenly flushed. "Ma'am, while you were getting dressed and putting up your hair, I took the mugs across the hall and rinsed them and then carried them up to the nursery. You didn't seem to need me to help you dress, and I thought you'd like to have everything nice and neat like when the doctor came—"

"It's all right," Laura soothed. "You and I just made the same mistake, a quite natural one."

"Exactly," Hugh Malverne said. He reached into his bag and brought out a prescription pad. "For the moment I think a glass of warm milk would be in order, or at least as much of it as she wants to drink. I'll also give you a prescription that you can have made up at a chemist's in the morning.

261

It will settle her stomach if she seems queasy or otherwise uncomfortable."

He was still writing when someone knocked sharply on the door of the adjoining room. Laura said, "Bessie, would you mind—"

Bessie went into Laura's room. There came the sound of Lady Parrington's agitated voice. Then she was in the child's room, a distraught, white-faced woman in pale yellow brocade with ostrich plumes of the same color in her elaborately coiffed hair. She cried, "Mrs. Mockton just told me—" She sat down on the bed and gathered the pale child into her arms. "Oh, Lily, Lily!"

Dr Malverne got to his feet. "Lady Parrington!" His voice was sharp. "Compose yourself! Don't agitate the child further. She needs to get back to sleep."

"You are right, of course." She lowered her grandchild gently to the pillow and then stood up. "But could you tell me—"

"Apparently it was some sort of food poisoning. Mrs. Parrington, fortunately, had an emetic on hand. Lily will be all right now. I've advised warm milk for the moment, and I'm leaving a prescription in case she feels any distress tomorrow." He looked at Bessie. "If you can bring the milk—"

"No!" Lady Parrington said. "I'll bring the milk. Bessie, I'm sure you are needed downstairs."

When the two women had left the room, Hugh smiled down at the child and then turned to Laura. "Could I speak to you alone for a moment?"

In Laura's room he said to her, "It's as unfortunate for you as for the little girl that this should happen right now, when you're already so run-down."

"I'll be all right."

"You will if you rest for several days."

He made no mention of the two-hundred-pound check he had given her or of Aggie Thompson. But she knew that in effect he was saying, "Don't pursue the matter with that old woman! Not until you've given yourself a chance to become thoroughly rested."

She said, "Thank you. Thank you again for getting here so soon tonight."

Usually when they parted he took her hand for a moment or two, but tonight, perhaps because he was aware of being in her bedroom, he did not touch her.

"Good night, Laura. Telephone me tomorrow and let me know how Lily is doing."

She accompanied him to the door and stood looking after him for a moment as he walked to the landing and started down the stairs. Then, just as she was about to close her door, she became aware that Clive Parrington, no longer in evening clothes, had emerged from his room. He walked toward her, carrying a valise that no doubt held the clothes he had worn at dinner.

He stopped. "How is Lily?"

"Then you heard about it?"

"Yes, Mrs. Mockton told us as soon as the other guests had left. I suppose she felt that since the child seemed to be in no danger, it would be best not to upset the entire party. How is Lily now?"

"She seems fine. Dr. Malverne says it must have been some sort of food poisoning."

"Oh."

They stood looking at each other. Then, to her dismay, she heard herself asking, "You're going to your club?"

"Yes." He stood there for another moment and then said, "Good night," and walked toward the stairs. She turned quickly and went back into her room.

She was in Lily's room, seated beside the bed of the now-drowsy child, when Lady Parrington knocked and then immediately came into the room. She carried a glass of milk in her hand. "My dear," she said to Laura, "may I—"

Laura got up from the chair. Lady Parrington sat down and with one arm raised the child to a sitting position and supported her. "Here, my darling, drink this for Grandmother. That's right, my dearest."

Laura looked down at the tender, still-lovely face. How ardent it was, she thought, this love that Dorothy Parrington had transferred from her dead son to that son's child.

Twenty-Five

LILY SEEMED QUITE recovered in the morning. Nevertheless, Laura insisted that she stay in bed. She herself still felt somewhat tired. At ten she telephoned Hugh Malverne, who said that since the child seemed to be doing so nicely it would not be necessary for her to take the medicine Martha had fetched from the chemist's earlier that morning. After that, she telephoned the League office to say that she would not be in.

Still later, Laura ate lunchon alone and then returned to Lily's bedside to read from *Alice*. When Lily's eyelids began to droop, Laura laid the book aside.

She was in her own room, with the door closed between herself and the napping child, when someone knocked. It was Lady Parrington, her manner both agitated and determined. As soon as they sat facing each other in armchairs drawn up to the unlighted fireplace, the older woman said, "I sent Cornelia down to Walmsley on the early morning train. She returned half an hour ago. She has made all the arrangements for us to go down there."

Laura said, puzzled, "You mean in August?"

"I mean *now*, or rather, tomorrow morning. Oh, it's not a good time for us to go for several reasons. For one thing, there's the Midsummer's Eve fair day after tomorrow."

"The fair?"

"The locals hold it every year on this heath about five miles from Walmsley. Jugglers and Morris dancers and pony races and all that. Then they build bonfires and stay out on the heath all night. The Sproggses always go. I don't want to risk losing them, and so I said in my message that they could go to the fair if they got everything ready for us ahead of time. But then there's the matter of Lily's room."

Laura said, bewildered, "Lily's room?"

"At Walmsley, I mean. I ordered it redone so that it would be a surprise for her when we go down in August. It must be thoroughly torn up right now. But that's no real problem. There are plenty of other rooms. Of course, Justin is quite another matter."

Laura said, increasingly at sea, "Justin?"

"I thought you would have heard. The silly boy was in his cups last night. In fact, he must have been drinking for some time before he came here for Joseph's birthday dinner. Anyway, when he went back to his flat he tripped on the stairs and cut his face badly. I went to see him this morning, and he looks dreadful. Just the same, we must go."

"To Walmsley? What do you mean by 'we'?"

"Just you, Cornelia, myself, and the child. Not Bessie. Mrs. Mockton's rheumatism is still bad, and she needs Bessie. We'll manage nicely without her."

"But *why?* Why do you want to go?"

"Because of Lily, of course." Dorothy Parrington's face turned a shade paler. "Do you realize that if you hadn't had that medicine on hand, the child might have died before you could have gotten help?"

It was a thought that Laura for the past fifteen hours or so had been trying not to dwell on. "Still, I don't see why—"

"*I want that child out of this house!*"

Laura felt a cold ripple down her spine. "Why? Food poisoning might happen any—"

"How do any of us know it was food poisoning? It could have been something else."

When Laura just stared at her, she went on, hands clenched in her lap, "Counting the servants, there were about twenty people moving about in this house last night. One of them could have slipped up the stairs and opened the door of this room without your knowing it. You could have been with Lily in her room."

She *had* been beside Lily's bed, she recalled now, when Bessie brought the cocoa. And she had gone on reading for quite a while after that. She thought of someone slipping into the little spirit stove in this room, dropping something into the mug ornamented with the dancing poodle—

No! No matter how much someone resented her or wanted to be rid of her, surely he or she would not attack her child.

And yet, there was that man who had

been following her. She had not seen him yesterday, but doubtless he had been somewhere around. Doubtless, too, he had reported—to Sir Joseph?—that she had gone to that pub near Billingsgate Wharf—

Panic began to swell inside her. "Perhaps Lily and I had best return to New York."

"No! Come to Walmsley first. We can relax there for a few days, then decide what's best to do—"

She reached over and grasped both of Laura's hands in her own. "I know I sound silly. I know she probably just picked up something somewhere, and then forgot that she had, or was afraid to admit that she had."

"Something?"

"Something in the kitchen, say. Mrs. Mockton told me that they had put something around to keep down the black beetles. Lily could have wandered into the kitchen. Everyone, including Bessie, was busy yesterday getting ready for the party.

"Please!" Her hands tightened around Laura's. "If you like, just think of it as indulging a silly old woman, but let's take Lily to Walmsley."

You're certainly not that old, Laura thought. And it was not Lady Parrington's agitation that made her consent. She too felt a need to get herself and her child out of this house. She realized that the sense of some sort of threat to Lily was absurd, but there it was.

"All right. We'll go."

Twenty-Six

LAURA AND LILY, along with Lady Parrington and Cornelia Slate, boarded an early train the next morning. Lily seemed to have recovered completely, so that she had to be restrained from leaving the compartment to explore the aisle. Cornelia Slate, her expression less aloof than usual, sat in the aisle corner of one of the seats and knitted. As for Laura, she responded as she usually did to the open countryside. When London's grimy outskirts were behind them, she began to relax. As she gazed out the window at lush fields dotted with grazing sheep, and at white plaster cottages with overhanging thatched roofs, she felt a sense of peace stealing over her.

Back there in London was a drink-soaked old woman waiting to tell her the lord only knew what once she cashed that two-hundred-pound bank draft still folded in her reticule. Back there, too, was that tall house with its withdrawn master, its ill-assorted half-brothers, neither of whom still lived beneath its roof, and its memories of still another brother, dead for many months now in a foreign land. Yes, she knew that all that was back there, waiting for her. But at the moment she was most aware of June sunlight, lying like a benediction on the serene English landscape.

Lady Parrington seemed unaffected by the day's beauty. Evidently too tense to take her knitting or crocheting from her work basket on the seat beside her, she sat with gloved hands clenched in her lap and her eyes fixed with an unseeing look on the fields sliding past.

Laura wondered what the older woman was thinking about. Her grandchild two nights ago, lying white and spent and with pupils so dilated that her eyes looked dark? The adored elder son she had lost? Perhaps, too, she was feeling guilt over her apparently much less beloved younger son, his face badly cut after a drunken fall.

Soon after they had luncheon in the dining car, the train reached the station three miles from Walmsley. The ancient but beautifully kept brougham was waiting for them, with Sproggs himself on the box. The regular coachman, he told them, had already started for the fair at Ainsworth Heath. "As I told Miss Slate, me and the missus will be starting out early in the morning."

Laura sensed beneath his deferential air a kind of guilty defiance. He felt uncomfortable that her Ladyship and the others were being left to shift for themselves. On the other hand, what right did her Ladyship have to come to Walmsley right now, when she knew that he and the missus always went to the fair?

The road to Walmsley, almost empty when Laura first traveled it, today was thronged with traffic, all going in the same direction. There were lumbering farm carts, and men on foot or on horseback who led strings of wiry-looking ponies, and multi-covered gypsy caravans with black-eyed children peering out over the tailgates. They were all going, Lady Parrington said, to Ainsworth Heath, where for centuries a fair had been held on the longest day and shortest night of the year. Fleetingly Laura wondered if, even back in the days when Stonehenge was built, people had gathered on Ainsworth Heath, not to race ponies, but to take part in the mysterious religious rites of the Druids.

Lily was asking, "Can't we go to the fair, too? Can't we?"

"No, darling," her grandmother answered. "The fair is for local people. Besides, you'll have Toby to ride, and there will be cherries to pick, and I'm sure that by now there will be ducklings on that pond behind the stables."

Laura said, "She's never ridden Toby without Zach leading him. Won't Zach be at the fair, too?"

"He hasn't gone to it for years. He told me that he can't hear the music and his stiff joints keep him from dancing, so what would be the use?"

A few minutes later she said, "Since we'll be shifting for ourselves, I asked Mrs. Sproggs to make up rooms for us on the ground floor, so that we'll be nearer the dining room and the kitchen. She said she would, didn't she, Cornelia?"

Cornelia nodded. "Of course."

Lady Parrington said to Laura, "There are only two adjoining bedrooms on the ground floor. One of them is the one I've occupied in the past when work was being done on the floor above. In fact, some of my things are kept there. So I asked Mrs. Sproggs to make up the adjoining room for Lily. Do you mind?"

With mingled pity and resentment, Laura thought, she doesn't trust me to guard my own child now. She wants Lily sleeping in the room next to *hers*. Aloud she said, "No, I don't mind."

They topped the last rise in the road. There, in its cup of low hills, stood Walmsley.

Dinner that night was both cooked and served by Mrs. Sproggs. Her manner, too, Laura observed, held guilty defiance. It was becoming increasingly evident that in England not even the rich and titled could prevail against centuries-old tradition. When she'd served the cherry cobbler, Mrs. Sproggs said, "Sproggs and I will leave early, your Ladyship. I'll make breakfast porridge before I go. All you'll need to do is reheat it. I'll bank the fire in the cookstove. It ought to last for hours. And you'll have the spirit stove in the kitchen. And if you want cold things for dinner, there's ham and pheasant in the larder."

Lady Parrington's voice was meek. "Thank you, Mrs. Sproggs. I'm sure we'll do nicely."

They all went to bed soon after dinner. In

the room adjoining Lady Parrington's larger one, Laura sat by her daughter's bed for a few minutes and read to her from *Huckleberry Finn*. Somewhat to Laura's chagrin, Lily did not seem to mind that her mother would not be sleeping in the next room. Rather she appeared to regard the temporary separation as a sign that she was growing up. Laura kissed her daughter's cheek, said good night to Lady Parrington, and went down the corridor to the room assigned to her.

Although smaller than the one she had occupied on the floor above, the room was pleasant, with a faded Aubusson carpet and several small still lifes of fruit and flowers on the paneled walls. The bed, too, was comfortable, and yet she could not sleep. She kept thinking of London: of Belle Mulroney and Billy Barker and that greedy crone in that Billingsgate pub. Most disturbing of all, she kept remembering Lily's small white face, filled with pain and terror. And she remembered how, later that night, she had seen Clive Parrington step from his room across the hall, his valise in his hand—

She commanded herself, Don't think about those things! She needed a few days' respite from the unanswered questions that plagued her. And perhaps here in the country, with their near loss of Lily bringing them closer together, she might in a little while feel that she could broach to her mother-in-law the exceedingly painful subject of Richard's banishment and death. Lady Parrington also might cast some light on her stepson's strange, ambivalent behavior—

Stop thinking, she again commanded herself. Just listen to the country sounds. Wind through the tall elms on Walmsley's south lawn. The distant hooting of an owl. The even more distant barking of some farm dog.

Too, there were the sounds made by this ancient house. In the cooling night air, stairs and floorboards creaked. Floors that had known the tread of plumed cavaliers, and fashionable rakes of George the Fourth's time, and, quite recently, the sweep of tilting hoop skirts.

Her thoughts blurred, and she slept.

Twenty-Seven

A KNOCK ON the door awoke her. The almost-level rays of the sun, striking through the east window, told her that it was still early. She called, "Come in."

Lady Parrington said, sounding embarrassed, "I'm afraid I can't open the door."

Laura swung out of bed, lifted her flower-print wrapper from a chair back, and put it on. She opened the door to find her mother-in-law standing in the hall. She wore a floor-length white apron over a dress of blue lawn. Her right hand was wrapped in a white kitchen towel, with her left hand holding the towel in place.

Laura said, opening the door wide, "What on earth!"

The older woman moved past her into the room. "I've done something absurd. I've cut my thumb. I wonder if you could help me take care of it."

"Of course!"

Lady Parrington said, as Laura poured water from the pitcher into the washstand basin, "I thought it best not to waken Cornelia. She's a good soul. I don't know what I'd do without her. But she's one of these people who turn giddy at the sight of blood."

Unwrapping the towel, Laura saw that the cut, a fairly deep one, still bled. "Hold your hand in the water for a little while, so that the wound will wash clean. How on earth did it happen?"

"I went down to the kitchen early this morning. I've always liked to cook. For a while when I was a young girl in this house, we had a very nice cook. Not short-tempered, the way so many of them are. She let me try my hand at baking little cakes. I thought I'd bake some spiced cakes for you and myself and some plain vanilla ones for Lily, since anything highly flavored might not be good for her after her upset. Anyway, I was chopping nuts for the cakes, and the knife slipped—"

"Oh, dear!"

"You see, I was hurrying. As soon as the cakes were in the oven—the Sproggses left the fire nicely banked, by the way—I planned to write a note to Justin so that Cornelia could take it to him on the early train. But now I won't even be able to write."

"Tell me what to say, and I'll write it for you."

"Oh, thank you, my dear. I've been worrying about Justin. He's always felt that I—I loved him so much less than I did Richard. And my running off to the country, right after he's had an accident, must reinforce that belief. In fact, he said something to that effect yesterday morning. He said that I

278

would never have deserted Richard if he had been hurt."

After a moment, she added, "Of course, he's been right about my feelings. I tried to love my sons equally, but Richard always had first place in my heart."

Not knowing what answer to make to that, Laura said, "I think we can bandage your thumb now."

She used a fresh linen handkerchief from her valise, tearing off its hem to tie around the bandage. She asked, "Does it hurt much?"

"It throbs a little, that's all. Now I think you'll find letter paper over there in the desk."

When Laura sat with pen poised, Lady Parrington dictated:

"My dearest child,
I can see how my leaving must seem to you a grievous wrong. But the reasons are overwhelming. It does not mean that I don't love you. I love you more than I do any living creature."

Lady Parrington said, "Just sign it 'Mother.' " Then, after a moment, "I think I'd better add a postscript."

Again she dictated:

"We'll be back in a few days, and then I will tell you why I felt it necessary to come to Walmsley for at least a little while. I didn't have time to go into the whole matter yesterday morning. And Justin, one thing more. I realize that this is no time to lecture you, but I must point out that you wouldn't have fallen if you hadn't drunk too much, which is something you do far too often. Please, my darling, take my words to heart."

Laura asked, when she had finished writing the last sentence, "Shall I address an envelope?"

"No need to address the envelope. Cornelia will take it to his flat and hand it to him. Thank you, my dear. Are you coming to breakfast now? I've had mine, but there is plenty of porridge left."

Laura glanced at the mantel clock. Still only five after six. "I think I'll try to sleep a little longer. And I don't think it would hurt Lily to sleep until eight. We can both have breakfast then."

"Splendid. That way Cornelia will have the kitchen all to herself to cook as big a breakfast as she likes. She deserves it, poor dear, with me keeping her on the run back and forth between here and London."

She left the room, carrying the note to her wine-bibbing son in her left hand and in the right the kitchen towel that she had wrapped around her wounded thumb.

At ten that morning, dressed in her mother-in-law's old riding habit, Laura stood with Zach in the stable yard. From behind the stables came the sound of Lily's high, gleeful voice and occasionally Lady Parrington's quieter one. Grandmother and grandchild were feeding bread to the ducks.

Half an hour earlier, Lady Parrington had stated firmly that there would be no need for Laura to return from her ride in order to prepare Lily's midday meal. She herself could manage that, in spite of her wounded thumb. After all, it was just a matter of placing on the table the cheese and sliced cold meat and fruit that Mrs. Sproggs had left in the larder. Aware that the truth was that Lady Parrington wanted Lily to herself for the day, Laura had agreed to make a luncheon ham sandwich and take it with her.

Now Zach said, tightening the saddle cinch

around Nell's fat belly, "Best you enjoy yourself while the day's still fine."

She looked up at the cloudless sky. She had learned that Zach could read lips, and so she said, forming the words carefully, "What do you mean? Why shouldn't it stay fine?"

"Fog's coming."

"Fog? How do you know?"

"I can smell it. If you'd been here as long as I have, you'd be able to smell it, too." He added sourly, "Those folks out on Ainsworth Heath ain't going to enjoy their all-night singing and dancing much. Likely they won't even be able to see each other." His voice held a distinct note of what the Germans call *Schadenfreude*, or pleasure in the misfortune of others.

She rode out across the low hills and then down the village high street. When she reached the church, she tied Nell to the hitching post and went up the walk.

As before, she found the church empty. And as before, she moved slowly down the aisles through the multicolored light, looking at the tombs of Calvertons, both those in the walls and those marked by slabs in the stone floor. Then, at the head of the main aisle, she stood still, frowning. Where was the tomb of Lady Parrington's grandfather,

Henry Calverton? If she remembered correctly, the brass plate in the Walmsley portrait gallery had indicated that he had lived from sometime around 1765 to early 1800s. There were several Henry Calvertons among the family members buried here during the last three hundred years, but none with those dates.

She went back along the aisles to make sure. Here was Josiah Calverton, 1730 to 1790. He must have been Lady Parrington's great-grandfather. Here was her father, Howard Calverton, 1800 to 1870. But there was no Henry Calverton between them.

Why? Laura found the question oddly troubling. She sat down in one of the pews and, for a minute or two, stared unseeingly at the pulpit.

Then the probable answer came to her. For some reason he had been buried not beneath this stone floor but out in the churchyard. She got up and went in search of the sexton.

She found him behind the church, leaning on his shovel beside a freshly dug grave. She marveled at the sturdiness of these country men, able to do such hard work at an obviously advanced age.

She said, "Good day. My name is Laura

Parrington. I'm Sir Joseph and Lady Parrington's daughter-in-law."

He gave her a gap-toothed smile. "That I know, ma'am. I'm Watts, Sam Watts."

"How do you do?" She hesitated and then said, "Would it be too much trouble for you to show me Henry Calverton's grave?"

"Which Henry, ma'am? Happen there's several of them buried here."

"I know. But I mean the one who is *not* buried in the church. He was born about 1765, I think, and died in 1802 or thereabouts. I imagine his grave must be here in the churchyard."

He stared at her. "The churchyard? Oh, no, ma'am."

"You mean he was lost at sea? Something like that?"

"Don't you know? Why, that Henry Calverton was buried in the prison yard at Newgate."

Standing there in the bright sunlight, with the scent of grass and wild flowers around her, it took her several seconds to absorb his words.

Newgate. She had a vague memory of hearing how, at times in the past, prisoners hung at Newgate were cut down and then buried within the prison walls.

284

She asked thinly, "But why? What had he done?"

"Killed somebody. What else, ma'am?"

"Who? Who was killed?"

"Ma'am, I can't rightly say. I wasn't even born yet when it happened."

She said good-bye and walked back to where she had tethered the gray mare. She rode on through the rolling countryside toward Bailey's Hill. What the old man had said weighed upon her more heavily than she could account for. After all, it had happened close to a hundred years ago.

But even though it was well in the past, she felt it might account for something that had puzzled her—Dorothy Calverton's marriage. She was well-born and rich and beautiful, and yet she had married a plain man of humble origin, a widower with an infant son. Could it be that most of the other county families had been unwilling to ally themselves with a family that had included an executed murderer? It seemed to Laura both unlikely and unfair, but it might have been the case.

When she reached the top of Bailey's Hill, she remained in the saddle for a moment, looking out across the downs to that stretch of bright water. Then she dismounted and tied Nell's reins to the oak sapling. Sitting down on the grass, she took from her skirt pocket the paper-wrapped ham sandwich she had made that morning.

The sound of a train whistle reached her, and she knew that the afternoon train from London was approaching the local station. Perhaps Cornelia Slate was aboard it, unless she intended to take the last train. Could it possibly be that Clive Parrington was aboard it, too? Her body tensed at the thought that soon she might see him riding toward her.

She finished her sandwich and lay back in the grass, gaze fixed on the tender blue sky. The minutes stretched out. Still there was no warning whinny from Nell, no grass-muffled thud of hoofs. Gradually she gave up the expectation of seeing Clive. Gradually, too, the sense of oppression induced by the sexton's words slipped from her. Eyes closed, at last she was aware only of the sun's warmth, and birdsong, and the smell of clover.

Without intending to, she must have slept for a while, because when she next opened her eyes the sun had traveled some distance toward the west. She stood up and shook out her skirts and then looked east toward the Channel.

She gave a startled exclamation. Although

the sun still shone down on Bailey's Hill, a wall of fog, the sullen dark blue of a bruise, had blotted out the horizon and that distant gleam of water. Coincidence? Or was Zach really capable of smelling a change in the weather?

She went on staring at the fog bank. It was more like a long, gigantic wave than a wall, she realized now, rolling over and over on itself without breaking into foam. And it was moving closer. Even though the sun was as bright here as ever, the temperature had begun to drop. It was as if cool, invisible fingers had been extended to brush her face, her hands.

Perhaps it was the memory of that fog-shrouded afternoon in Bostwick Square. Whatever the reason, she suddenly felt uneasy. She untethered Nell and mounted.

The fog, not very heavy at first, began to eddy around her as she neared the village. It was still not like London fog, with its admixture of coal smoke, as she rode down the high street. But even so, it was thick enough that the lamps had been lighted behind both cottage and shop windows.

By the time she reached the rough stretches of road beyond the village, the fog was so thick that she feared that at any moment

Nell might step into a hole and break her leg. The mare seemed to share her anxiety because her pace, slow at any time, had became glacial. She seemed to hesitate before she put each hoof down. At last, through a rent in the fog, Laura saw the dim bulk of Walmsley. She was glad to see it, and yet somehow the sight of it brought back that sense of oppression that the sexton's words had awakened in her.

Zach was waiting for her in the stable yard. "Didn't I tell you, ma'am?" he greeted her. "Won't be able to see their hands before their faces, they won't, up on Ainsworth Heath."

Twenty-Eight

SHE WAS ABOUT to change from her riding habit when someone knocked on the door of her room. Knowing that it must be either Lady Parrington or Cornelia, Laura called, "Come in."

Lady Parrington said, walking into the room, "That beastly fog! I'm sorry your ride was spoiled."

"It wasn't. The day was lovely until a couple of hours ago."

"Well, after you change, come down to the little parlor. It's opposite the dining room, you know. Sproggs had laid a fire in there, and I thought it would be a cheerful place for tea on a day like this. And by the way, I baked those spice cakes after all."

Laura glanced at the older woman's bandaged thumb, "How did you manage that?"

"It was a simple matter. The batter was already mixed before I cut my hand. All I had to do was spoon the batter onto the baking tin. Besides, Lily helped me. She loved doing it. More and more that child reminds me of myself when I was small."

"Has she been good?"

"As gold. But then, she always is."

Laura considered that point debatable but refrained from saying so.

"She's already had her supper. Right now she's playing with the Japanese garden."

Laura said, dismayed, "You don't mean the one from the étagère in the drawing room!" Far from being a toy, the miniature reproduction was a work of art—a Japanese temple and teahouse, both of exquisite porcelain, a porcelain bridge, and several dwarfed fruit and evergreen trees, all set on a tray of red and gold lacquer. "She might break those lovely things, you know."

"Why, Lily never breaks anything."

Oh, yes, she does, Laura thought, but again refrained from speaking.

"Well, my dear, come down for tea as soon as you are ready."

A few minutes later, Laura walked down the corridor. She paused briefly to look at the disquieting sight of her daughter seated on the floor, surrounded by scattered porcelain miniatures worth hundreds of pounds. After cautioning her to be careful, she went on down the hall to the "small parlor," a room that really was small compared with most in this house. Today, with a fire snapping in the grate and the dark red velvet curtains drawn against the fog-shrouded outer world, the parlor looked cozy and inviting.

There were only two cups on the table. Laura asked, "Where is Cornelia? Isn't she well?"

"Oh, I suppose I didn't tell you. I decided to tell her that she could stay overnight in London. It really didn't seem fair to ask her to make the round trip in a few hours, when she'd done so only the day before yesterday."

They sat beside the fire while Lady Parrington poured the tea and then extended a plate of little flat cakes. Laura took a bite of one. "Delicious," she said, and hastily swallowed some tea.

Lady Parrington frowned at the cake from which she had just taken a bite. "You don't think I put in too much ginger?"

"Oh, no!" To emphasize the point, Laura swallowed the rest of the confection in her hand.

Smiling now, Lady Parrington extended the plate. "Have another. Take two. They're really quite small."

Laura did so. Feeling she had done more than her duty, she declined a fourth. Lady Parrington said, "Now tell me about your ride."

"Well, I stopped by the village church—" She broke off, hearing in her mind's ear the old sexton's voice: "Killed somebody. What else, ma'am?"

She thought, Why not ask her about her grandfather? After all, she need not tell the truth if she doesn't want to. She can say that he was lost at sea, or that his body was never recovered from some battlefield of the Napoleonic Wars, or something of the sort.

She said, "I couldn't find your grandfather's grave, either in the church or outside it."

For a moment Lady Parrington sat with

her teacup suspended in her left hand. Then she set it down in its saucer. "I just assumed Richard had told you. But since he hasn't, I had better."

Even though she herself had broached the subject, Laura shrank back from hearing what the other woman might say. "If it's something you would rather not—"

"You're part of the family. You have a right to know. Henry Calverton was hanged."

The domesticity of the setting—the drawn curtains, the snapping fire, the tea table—seemed to make her words doubly chilling.

"He killed someone. A young woman, the daughter of one of his tenants. Walmsley had several tenant farms in those days."

Laura managed to say, "But why did he—"

"No reason. No rational reason. It was a kind of madness that came upon him sometimes. In—in his intimate relations with women he was sometimes overwhelmed by a need to—to give pain. This time he went too far. The young woman died."

Laura's hands flew up to cover her face. She said in a muffled voice, "How dreadful!"

"Yes, dreadful." The older woman's voice

was flat. "Dreadful for everyone, including those who were born years after it happened."

Laura took her hands down from her face and clenched them in her lap. Lady Parrington, she saw, was staring into the fire. Laura felt she must be thinking of her own youth, and of how that murder had outweighed her beauty and her lineage, so that she had had no recourse except a marriage that otherwise would have been considered a misalliance.

Her words seemed to confirm Laura's guess. "County families remember things for years, decades, generations."

"I'm sorry, so terribly sorry, that I caused you to talk about it."

"I'm sure you would have learned of it sooner or later." Then, her eyes searching Laura's face, "You don't look well, my dear. Has learning about my grandfather upset you that much?"

"I—I don't know. Maybe it's just that I stayed out too long today." Suddenly she was aware of fatigue, a leaden heaviness throughout her body.

"Why don't you go to your room and lie down until dinner?"

"But there's Lily. I must see that she gets to bed—"

"I can do that. Go lie down. Try to nap if you can. And try not to think of what I just told you. After all, it happened long, long ago."

"Perhaps I had better rest." Suddenly eager to escape this warm little room that only a few minutes ago had seemed so pleasant, she got to her feet.

Twenty-Nine

SOMEONE WAS KNOCKING.

Aroused from troubled sleep, she found that she was lying fully clothed on her bed. The glow of the bedside lamp filled the room. Groggily, she recalled that she had lit the lamp after she had returned from her ride and had left it burning when she went to tea in the small parlor.

The mantel clock chimed eight. But eight in the morning or eight at night? In either case, it should be light outside, but the window with its undrawn draperies framed darkness. Oh, yes. The fog.

Again someone knocked. Laura swung her feet off the bed and sat up. How very tired she still felt. "Come in," she called.

The door swung open. Lady Parrington

pushed a tea cart into the room, her bandaged right thumb held upright from the handle bar. "Since you're not feeling well, I decided we'd have dinner in your room."

Dinner. So it was still evening. "Oh, you shouldn't have. Your hand—"

"Nonsense. It was easy. I just used the spirit stove to heat the soup Mrs. Sproggs left. Since it's mulligatawny, I felt it would be sufficient for our entire meal."

"I'm sure it will." In fact, Laura felt that after the spice cakes she could have done nicely with no dinner at all. "Is Lily—"

"She's in bed and asleep. I left her door into the hall open in case she wakes up and calls for us. Now, my dear, would you fetch me a folding table? You'll find several in a small closet three doors down the hall."

"Of course." Laura shivered, then crossed her arms in front of her.

"Yes, it's cold," Dorothy Parrington said. "That beastly fog. While you're fetching the table, I'll light the fire."

Laura found the closet with a stack of card tables standing on edge. She took the outermost one. It was made of some wood light in both color and weight, and yet it felt heavy in her hand. She thought, what's wrong with me? I've never had the aftereffects of a cold last this long.

By the time she returned to her room, the first flames were licking at the small logs one of the Sproggses had lain in the gate. Laura set up the table between the two small fireside armchairs. Then she said, "I still feel only half awake. Do you mind if I take a few seconds to freshen up?"

"Of course not. The soup will stay hot."

At the washstand Laura poured water into the big bowl of white china, splashed her face, and dried it. Then she poured water into the glass beside the bowl and drank it. Sensing that in a few minutes she would feel thirsty again, she refilled the glass and carried it to the table with her.

Lady Parrington ladled soup from a cream-colored tureen into soup bowls. She had been right about the soup's remaining hot. Heavily spiced with curry, it was also hot in the other sense of the word. At Lady Parrington's urging, Laura managed to finish the soup in her bowl, taking sips of water between spoonfuls.

There were white grapes for dessert. Grateful for their cool, delicate flavor after the curried soup, Laura ate a small bunch. "Tea? Coffee?" Lady Parrington asked. "I didn't make any because I thought we would both sleep better without it. But it would be no trouble to—"

"Oh, no, thank you."

Lady Parrington leaned back in her chair, her face suddenly grave. "Very well, then. Laura, I have something to tell you about Richard."

Laura found that, despite the fire's heat, she felt more chilled than ever. She also realized that for the second time in a few hours she was afraid to hear what her mother-in-law was about to tell her.

"Richard inherited more than his handsome appearance from his great-grandfather."

Suddenly Laura found it hard to breathe. She said, "I don't know what—"

"I think you do know." The woman's voice was weighted with sorrow. "Oh, I don't think you had any inkling of it before I told you about Henry Calverton this afternoon. I think my son must have loved you very much, my dear. So much that he would have done anything to keep you from knowing the truth about him. In fact, in the end—"

She broke off. Laura's hands clutched the arms of her chair. Something odd seemed to be happening to Lady Parrington's face. In the wavering firelight it appeared to grow closer, then recede.

"It must have started after he entered Cambridge. Somehow he discovered that in Ely or other surrounding towns there were women who, if sufficiently well paid, would accommodate men like him. But it wasn't until he'd left Cambridge and had joined his father's firm that one night he—went too far. And it wasn't until then that his father and I found out what he was."

She went on, describing how she had been awakened one midwinter night by her husband and her deathly pale son. A woman was dead. Strangled. Richard had not meant to hurt her that much. And then he realized he had.

"He told us a little about her. She was a woman of forty-odd who had lived with her mother in a Spitalfields slum. Their name was Thompson, Aggie and May Thompson. May had been a street walker since the age of fourteen. It was then that her mother had sold her to some man for two pounds. May continued to make her living from men. Her mother had of recent years been a night charwoman at Waterloo Station.

"Richard wanted to turn himself over to the police. It was I who saw to it that he didn't. I told him that if he did, I—I would refuse to go on living.

"By that time my husband had awakened Clive. At first Clive said that the police must be told, no matter what the cost to all of us. I told him, just as I had Richard, that if that happened I would—end my own life. Evidently he saw I meant it, because he began to discuss with my husband what should be done. They finally decided to go to Spitalfields and—and wait for the dead woman's mother to come home from work.

"They walked about a quarter of a mile from Bostwick Square, engaged a hansom cab, and dismissed it quite a way from the address Richard had given them."

Through a ringing that had begun in her ears, Laura listened to the woman's voice. It too seemed to swell and then recede. She pictured the two men making their way across nighttime London, then climbing stairs to a room above a darkened shop. The dead woman was there, lying on the bed. A lamp was burning on an upended crate that served as a nightstand. They waited for the mother's return. With numb horror Laura thought of what the waiting time must have been like for Clive and his father.

"It was January, and daybreak came late,"

Lady Parrington said. "It was still dark when Aggie Thompson came home. My—my husband seized her as she came in the door and held his hand over her mouth. Clive took out his wallet. She—she understood. When my husband released her, she didn't scream.

"It was Clive who had suggested that they offer her a pound a month for the rest of her life. If offered a lump sum, she might accept it and then go straight to the police. But if she knew that a small but steady income would cease once she broke her silence, she would not break it.

"They coached her in her story. She must tell the police that as she approached the building where she and her daughter lived, she had seen a man run from it. By the light of the streetlamp she had seen that he was tall, forty-five or perhaps older, and had graying dark hair. Furthermore, they told her, she must tell the police that she had recognized him as a regular customer of her daughter's but didn't know his name or anything else about him."

Lady Parrington said, "It—it worked out as we had hoped. Richard was never a suspect. As far as we know, no one was ever arrested for the crime. I don't suppose the police worked very hard on the case, a woman

300

like that. Just the same, Clive insisted that Richard leave England and stay away. If he remained here, sooner or later he might— might do something that would remind someone of how the Thompson woman had died."

Laura was shivering again, despite the fire's heat. She wrapped her arms around herself. And so he came to America, she thought, and he fell in love with me, and I with him. And he cherished me, protected me, guarded me against that dark and terrible side of his nature. In fact, probably at first he hoped that being in love had—cured him.

It had not. But when the urge, not just to possess a woman but to cause her pain, overwhelmed him, he sought out some other woman. One woman or many? Because of the steadily rising size of the withdrawals in that bank book, she thought it was probably one woman, a woman who had charged increasing sums for her compliance. And finally, perhaps because of growing despair, or a growing fear that once again, as in London, he might lose control completely, he had taken his own life.

She had no doubt now that it had been suicide, not robbery and murder. He had disposed of his watch and wallet somewhere, probably the East River, and then had climbed up to the el platform and walked out along its tracks—

She recalled how, when she looked at the withdrawals in that savings account book, it had occurred to her that Richard might have had some enemy, someone who was bleeding him dry. She had been right about that. Her handsome, gentle, boyish husband had had an enemy, an implacable one within him. And finally that enemy had demanded his life.

Again she was thirsty. Feeling lightheaded, she went to the washstand. She filled her glass, drained it, then carried the refilled glass back to her chair.

Lady Parrington said in a sorrowing voice, "Oh, my dear. How I wish you had never come to London."

Laura wished it, too, wished that at whatever cost she had managed to support herself and her child in New York and thus remained forever in ignorance of what her husband had been.

Nausea in the pit of her stomach now. The spice cakes? The curried soup? Or just the things she had heard?

From somewhere in the distance, fog-muffled, came the sound of the last train of the day from London, the one that Cornelia Slate would not be on, after all.

"But you did come here," Lady Parrington said. "From the moment your cable arrived, saying you had booked passage, I was literally ill with fear."

"Fear?" Laura felt not only nausea but a sharp pain in her stomach. She drained her glass.

"Fear that you would somehow learn the truth and thus threaten all we had managed to preserve of our son, his good name. Oh, we had been protecting the whole family's reputation, of course. But it was chiefly Richard that I was thinking of." Her voice became passionate. "I wanted everyone to remember him as handsome and charming and kind. Oh, with a weakness for gambling, of course. But I wanted that to be his only weakness in the minds of others.

"And I was right to be afraid of your coming. Somehow that dreadful hag, May Thompson's mother, heard you were here. She came and talked to you through the park fence—"

Lady Parrington broke off. Laura was aware of the woman's eyes looking at her keenly through the firelight. "How do you feel?"

"Not—well."

"Perhaps you'd better get yourself some more water."

Laura tried to rise. When she was halfway out of her chair, her legs buckled and she fell back. "I don't know what—"

"I'll get it for you." Rising, the woman filled the glass at the washstand and brought it back to place it beside Laura's soup bowl. Laura drank greedily.

Again seated in the other armchair, Lady Parrington said, "I knew you were uncomfortable, living with people who made it obvious you were not wanted. I felt that no matter how brave and stubborn you were, you would take yourself and your child away if you were sufficiently frightened. And so the next day, when you went out into the fog, I decided to take advantage of the opportunity."

Laura had a sense of unreality, as if it were only in a dream that she sat in a firelit room with pain spreading inside her and, a few feet away, her mother-in-law watching her from still-lovely blue eyes.

"You mean it was you?" Laura's tongue felt thick. "There in the park?"

"In a way it was quite simple. I already had a key to the gate in my room, but it

304

turned out to be unneeded because you had left the gate unlocked. The risky part was getting out of the house and then back in unobserved. True, I was sure that at that hour the chances were overwhelming that the lower hall would be empty. Joseph and Clive were at their offices. Bessie and Lily were up in the nursery. As for Cornelia, I'd told her that I wanted to take a long nap and would prefer that she go to her room. And the servants would be below stairs, busy with dinner preparations. Still, there was a slight chance of being seen. But it was a chance I felt I had to take since such an opportunity might never come again."

She broke off. Her gaze went to the fire, where one of the small logs had almost burned through in the middle. Then she said, "No one was in the lower hall. I took a straight-handled umbrella from that brass stand beside the door and carried it, still furled, of course, across the street. I—I didn't want to do you a grave injury, just one sufficient to make you decide to go back across the Atlantic. I hit you over the head and then went back across the square. Then came the frightening part. It would have been bad enough if someone had seen me leaving the house on a day like that. But if someone had seen me coming back in, the umbrella in my hand—

"The lower hall was empty. I put the umbrella back in the stand and climbed the stairs to my room."

The log in the grate collapsed, sending up sparks. Lady Parrington said, "And then the next day something happened that I had been avoiding. I saw Lily, my Richard's child." Her voice broke. "From then on, the last thing I wanted was for you to take her back to New York. But I also wanted more than ever that her father's name remain—unsullied.

"And your behavior was anything but re-assuring, Laura. Thanks to Dr. Malverne, you started going to the Working Women's League in Spitalfields several times a week. And finally you learned about Belle Mulroney and her daughter—"

Laura said, with an effort, "Valerie Lockwood mentioned her to me. But I thought that probably you didn't even know about Belle and her child."

"Oh, I knew! I knew when Richard's father gave him a thousand pounds to—to pay the Mulroney girl off. Anyway, you questioned Clive about her, and Clive told his father, and Joseph and I decided it might be wise to take you and Lily down here to Walmsley for a while. But it didn't seem to distract you from—from trying to find out about Richard's past. In fact, you seemed more determined than ever."

Determined. Into her increasingly clouded mind came the memory of Bailey's Hill, and Clive Parrington's prolonged, hungry kiss, and then his harsh voice saying, "I still want you to go home." Yes, she had been determined. Determined to find out what stood between her and Clive Parrington.

"My husband hired someone to watch you. We knew when you went back to that music hall. And we knew when you went to that pub near the Billingsgate Wharf and talked to Aggie Thompson. And then you went to Hugh Malverne's office. Aggie Thompson had asked for money in exchange for information, hadn't she? You went to Dr. Malverne to borrow it. Isn't that right?"

"Yes." Laura's lips felt numb, and her vision had begun to blur. "She wanted two hundred pounds. He gave me a bank draft. I was going to cash it the next day."

"Joseph thought that might be it. I knew then that something drastic had to be done." She paused for a long moment. "I use belladonna. It makes the eyes more beautiful, you know. I waited until Bessie, who was helping serve at my husband's birthday dinner that night, disappeared from the dining room about eight-thirty. She'd been there during the soup course, but not for the fish course. I knew she must have gone upstairs to remove your supper tray and put the cocoa mugs on the little spirit stove in your room. I excused myself and slipped upstairs. I was in luck. When I tapped very softly on the door of your room, you didn't answer. I was sure then that you must be reading aloud to Lily in her room. It took me only a second or two to open the door and empty the bottle of belladonna into the cocoa."

Laura thought laboriously, either I have gone mad, or she has. She couldn't have done that to her granddaughter. She loves her, to the point of adoration.

She moved her numb lips. "Are you saying that you poisoned Lily?"

"Of course not! You poisoned her. *You*. I was careful to put the poison in the plain mug, not that old one of Richard's with the dancing poodle on it. *You're* the one who almost killed her. You gave her the wrong mug."

Laura's increasingly numbed mind fumbled with the appalling thought. Yes, she decided, she must have made the mistake. She'd been still suffering from the after-effects of her cold and had still been upset over her talk with Aggie Thompson.

And if she had not made that mistake? If she, rather than Lily, had swallowed the poisoned cocoa, she in all probability would have died. Sleeping a child's sound sleep, Lily would not have heard her mother's moaning, as Laura had heard her daughter's. Nor would Laura's poison-clouded mind have remembered the ipecac.

Laura had read somewhere that if a belladonna victim did not get rid of the poison fast, paralysis usually resulted. She would have been unable to move or even cry out—

Lady Parrington said, "I think I heard something in the hall. Will you go and look, Laura?"

Befuddled, Laura tried to fulfill the request. She struggled to her feet, swayed giddily, and collapsed back into the chair. Lady Parrington stood up. She walked to the door, turned the key in the lock, then dropped the key into the bosom of her dress. She said, as she walked back to her chair, "Not that I think you would be able to get as far as the door, or the window, either. And even if you did, there's a stout copper screen on the window. All the ground floor windows were screened two years ago."

Laura said, "Was it—the soup?"

"No, the spice cakes. Arsenic works more slowly than the poison in belladonna. Zach told me that the poison he puts out for stable rats takes hours." She paused. "A few of the little cakes were all right, of course. I was careful to eat only those."

Laura's lips felt made of wood. "Why?"

"Why have I done this? I've told you why! I will not allow you to blacken Richard's memory. You seemed determined that, one way or another, you would learn the truth, and I was just as determined to keep it hidden. Not just for my dead son's sake. For my grandchild's sake, too."

"I meant, why—why have you told me—"

A kind of uncertainty came into the older woman's face. "Perhaps because I don't want you to think—I mean, I want you to know that I *had* to do this. You made it necessary. You with your stubbornness that just wouldn't give in."

The pain in Laura's stomach, only intermittent stabs moments before, had become like a giant hand, steadily squeezing her vitals. She gathered all her ebbing energies.

"You must get help for me right away,"

she said. "Not just for my sake. For yours. If I had died in the London house, there would have been others to blame. Quite a few others because of the party."

She paused, gasping for breath, and then went on, "But here you are the only one who could have done it. They won't hang you, I suppose. But they'll shut you up for a long time, maybe for life, in a prison or an asylum."

"No, my dear, they won't." There was no triumph in her voice. A kind of sadness, if anything. "You see, I have not acted too hastily, as I did the night of the birthday dinner. This time I've made sure that everything will go smoothly. There is your suicide note, for instance."

"My—my—"

"The one you wrote for me this morning because I had cut my thumb. The one that starts out, 'My dearest child, I can see how my leaving must seen to you a grievous wrong—"

Laura said, after a long, befuddled moment, "I wrote that note so that Cornelia could take it to Justin! You call him by name in the note. You mention his accident, and his drinking. So how could anyone possibly think—"

"All of that was in the postscript. The note itself makes no mention of Justin. It's only four sentences long, and it's signed 'Mother.' Now that I've cut off and burned the postscript, the note will serve nicely. I'll just place it on the stand beside your bed."

Laura's numbed mind struggled to frame a response to that but could not.

"I did not send Cornelia to London to take any kind of message to Justin. I sent her with some new instructions for the people who are starting to redecorate the drawing room. There was no need to send her to Justin. As far as I know, my son is perfectly well."

"You—you were lying about his having had a fall—"

Lady Parrington nodded. "As I told you, I took the time to think everything through. In fact, the idea that I might have to do something like this must have been at the back of my mind for some time. I think that is why I had you buy the arsenic that went into the spice cakes."

Despite the pain gripping her, Laura was able to think, She *is* mad. I bought no arsenic.

"As for the Sproggses' absence—well, the fact that they would be away at this particular time played into my hands. But if that had not been the case, I would have contrived some other means of making sure you and I were alone in the house. Except for the child, of course."

Lily, asleep in her room down the hall. Lily, who could not help her.

No one could help her. There was no one else within miles, except for Zach in his bed in the stable loft. Zach, who was deaf as a post and separated from her by hundreds of feet of stable yard that her poison-wracked body would never be able to cross, even if she did somehow manage to get out of this room.

I'm going to die, she thought. My little girl will be left in the care of the woman who killed me. And Clive and I will never have each other.

"You had best lie down on the bed, my dear." Lady Parrington said it quietly, even gently. "Try to stand up."

Laura did try to stand, but not so as to cross to the bed. She still had some tiny hope that she might wrest the key from the other woman, get to the door, and somehow—somehow—

But she found herself immobilized. She was able to put her hands on the chair's

313

arms but could not exert enough pressure to lift herself even an inch.

She became dimly aware that Lady Parrington had moved the table and now stood in front of her, hands under her armpits. She felt herself being lifted to her feet, being dragged, toes scraping over the carpet, by this woman who was shorter than herself and several pounds lighter and about twenty-five years older. She heard panting breath and after a moment realized that it was not her own but that of the woman who had dragged her across the firelit room toward the bed.

Sounds. Not just the woman's ragged breath, nor the hiss of logs in the fireplace, but sounds from beyond the door of this room. Running footsteps. A voice calling her name. The hands dragging her across the room loosened their grasp, and she dropped to the floor.

Thirty

FOR A TIMELESS interval after that, it seemed to Laura that everything had the disjointed quality of a dream. There was a shattering sound—someone's shoulder breaking the door?—and a woman's scream. Not hers, someone else's. Then somehow she was lying on the bed, and faces looked down at her through light that seemed to dim and then grow bright and then dim again. Clive's face, and Cornelia Slate's, and the round, vaguely familiar face of some man—oh, yes, Mr. Proudfoot, the chemist in the village. He was speaking to her. His voice, like the light, seemed to fluctuate, now loud, now soft, so that it was hard to understand him.

"Try to tell me, Mrs. Parrington! What have you swallowed?"

She tried to speak, but no sound came. She shook her head.

Mr. Proudfoot seemed to disappear. Now only Clive's white, frightened face and Cornelia's dismayed one looked down at her. But Mr. Proudfoot had not left the room. She heard him saying, "Lady Parrington! What has she swallowed? Was it that skin-rash remedy I made up earlier this. month? Was it? Lady Parrington! You must answer me."

With an effort, Laura turned her head so that she could see the fireplace. If her mother-in-law had been the one who screamed, she was screaming no longer. She sat in one of the armchairs. Her white face was empty, holding neither fear, nor rage, nor regret, not anything at all.

Frowning, he walked back to the bed. Laura's confused, groping thoughts found a memory, seized it. Dorothy Parrington saying, "I think that is why I had you buy the arsenic that went into the spice cakes."

Then it must be that Mr. Proudfoot had made the right guess. It *was* the compound he made up that had gone into the little cakes. At the request of her mother-in-law, Laura had bought the remedy in his shop.

Frantically, she tried to tell him so, but all she could do was to form the word *yes* with her lips.

After a moment he asked sharply, "You mean it *was* the skin-rash compound?"

She nodded.

He whirled around, all brisk authority now. "Mr. Parrington, take your mother out of here. Better to lock her in somewhere." He lifted a leather bag onto the bedside table and opened it. "Miss Slate, I want that basin brought over here, and the water pitcher and a glass. I want you or Mr. Parrington to bring me blankets. And I want milk, raw eggs—"

There seemed to be a brief gap in her consciousness after that. Then she smelled ipecac and saw the spoon held out to her. She took one spoonful, then another. For a few moments longer she knew only pain, and a chill that kept her shivering despite the blankets they had spread over her. Then she leaned above the basin placed on the floor beside the bed, and the deadly stuff gushed from her.

Thirty-One

IT WAS ALMOST July now, and the day was warm. They rode slowly toward Bailey's Hill, Laura on Nell, Clive on the big chestnut horse that he kept tightly reined, forcing it to keep to the venerable mare's pace. Laura wore not Lady Parrington's old habit but one borrowed from Cornelia Slate. Partly because of the weight Laura had lost during the five days since she had swallowed that arsenic compound, the habit fitted her even more loosely than the other one had. Still, she was glad not to be wearing Dorothy Parrington's clothes.

She did not like to think of her mother-in-law, that woman who had screamed in despair as her stepson's shoulder had shattered the door, then fallen as silent as if she had been born mute. She had not spoken the next day when, as Laura lay semiconscious in her room, Sir Joseph had come to Walmsley from London. She did not speak during the twenty-four hours it took her husband and stepson to decide what was to be done. And according to Sir Joseph, she had not opened her lips as he traveled with her, in the Walmsley carriage with the Calverton coat of arms on its door, to a place in Surrey, an establishment that called itself a hospital for nervous complaints. At last report she still remained mute.

Although she tried not to think of her mother-in-law, Laura did not hate her. After all, Dorothy Parrington had not acted out of hate. She had acted out of fear and out of a desperate need to protect her dead son from the world's scorn and outrage. In short, she had acted out of a kind of love, a fanatical, disproportionate love, but still love.

And Laura could understand that because she had loved Richard too. Oh, not all of Richard, of course. Not that dark madness he had successfully hidden from her. But she had loved the handsome and gentle Richard whom so many people, including Cornelia Slate, had found overwhelmingly attractive.

Now she thought, as the two horses started

up the daisy-starred slope of Bailey's Hill, I owe my life to Cornelia Slate.

It was Cornelia who had seen Dorothy Parrington deliberately cut her own thumb.

Laura now knew that early that morning, with old Zach already waiting to drive her to the station, Cornelia had gone below stairs. She wanted to make sure that she understood one small point in the instructions she was to pass along to the redecorators in the London house. As she moved along a passageway that connected the larder with the kitchen, she saw her employer standing at the big chopping block, a butcher knife upraised. Evidently her concentration on what she intended to do was so grim and total that she did not hear Cornelia's approach. She brought down the knife.

It had been Cornelia, not Lady Parrington, who gave a small scream.

The older woman whirled around, knife still in her left hand, and stared at Cornelia for a moment. Then she looked down at her right thumb, which was beginning to ooze blood. "What a clumsy creature I am. No, no, Cornelia. I can manage." She opened a drawer, took out a kitchen towel, and wrapped it around her injured hand. "Now go on, this minute. Don't miss your train. If you do, I'll be very cross."

Confused, not quite able to believe what she had seen, Cornelia had gone out to the waiting carriage. But as the train carried her toward London, her worry grew. She was becoming almost certain that Lady Parrington *had* cut her own thumb. And for the next twenty-four hours, Laura Parrington and her little girl would be alone in that house with a woman who, very probably, had performed an obviously irrational act.

But out of long obedience to a generous employer, she went to the house in Bostwick Square and passed along Lady Parrington's amended instructions to the decorators. As the day lengthened, though, her anxiety increased. Finally, in midafternoon, she telephoned Clive Parrington at his office. He came to the house at once.

"As soon as Cornelia told me what she had seen," Clive said three days later as he sat at Laura's bedside in Walmsley, "I knew that we should get to you as soon as possible. You see, I'd been uneasy ever since the night Lily was taken ill. I'd kept thinking, what if it *wasn't* food poisoning. And also I thought of what I'd heard about poisoners—that once they start, they keep on."

In fact, he had been so worried that he had tried to call Hugh Malverne to ask the doctor to accompany them on the train to Walmsley. The telephone had been answered by Malverne's manservant, who always took messages when the doctor was unavailable. Dr. Malverne, the man said, had gone to Richmond on a maternity case. It was than tha Clive had thought of Mr. Proudfoot. As a compounder of all sorts of preparations, from pest eradicaters to hair dyes to the arsenic preparations women took to improve their complexions, Mr. Proudfoot knew all about poisons—and their antidotes.

From the village train station Clive and Cornelia had hurried through the thinning fog to Mr. Proudfoot's shop. In his upstairs living quarters the chemist had been about to go to bed. But when he heard Cornelia's story he packed his leather valise with remedies he thought he might need. In the stable behind his house he backed his horse between the traces of his buggy, and then drove with Clive and Cornelia to Walmsley.

Now Clive said, studying her as she sat perched on Nell's broad back, "You're looking better. You have some color in your cheeks."

"I'm feeling better, much better."

"What were you thinking about just moments ago?"

"Mr. Proudfoot. You said he promised to keep quiet about what—what your stepmother tried to do. Do you think he will keep his words?"

"I hope so. But who can say for sure?"

"Just so his—his talking won't mean she'll be brought to trial."

"It won't, not unless you bring charges. Even then she would probably be judged unfit to stand trial."

"I'd hate to have her brought into court. I'd even begun to be a little fond of her, if only because she was so enchanted with Lily."

Clive said soberly, "I've been fond of her, too. More than fond. After all, she is the only mother I can remember. And even though from the time Richard was born he obviously meant more to her than every other human being in the world put together, she tried to be fair, tried to keep me, her stepson, from feeling shut out. That was why, when she threatened to kill herself if Richard were handed over to the police, I gave up all idea of doing anything except to try to protect him. And even though he resented my insistence that he leave England, I think that both he and his mother realized that he would be safer out of reach of the London police."

"Would you have gone on keeping his secret, even from me?"

"I don't know. Perhaps not. I'd fallen so deeply in love with you, you know."

She smiled. Yes, she knew. She had known long before the previous night, when, as they strolled over the south lawn after dinner, he has asked her to marry him. With perhaps unladylike promptness, she had replied that she certainly would.

"And yet," Clive went on, "I didn't feel that I could marry you or anyone while I was keeping it a secret that my father and I had covered up that—that poor harlot's death. Then, too, I felt horror at the thought of telling you that the man who'd been your husband for seven years—and so I wanted you to go far away, so that in time I might be able to forget you."

She said softly, "But I was stubborn."

He smiled. "Extremely stubborn."

When they reached the crest of the hill, they dismounted and looked across the downs at that distant shining. "That is the Channel, isn't it?"

"Yes."

For a while there was no sound except the

sough of wind through the young oak trees. Then he said, "Have you thought any more about Southampton?"

He meant the idea he had broached the night before about his taking over the Southampton office of Parrington Limited so that they would be well away not only from Walmsley but from that house in Bostwick Square as well.

"Yes," she said, "I think I'd like Southampton."

"I'm sure you will. The south coast of England is beautiful." After a moment he added, "This wind is strong. Are you getting cold?"

"No. I love this wind." She could feel it flattening her riding habit against her, blowing cool against her face and through her hair. "I like to think that right now it's blowing through our lives."

He looked down at her. "Blowing things back into the past?"

She nodded. "All the sad, mad things."

"So that we can start clean. Exactly," he said, "exactly."

A note on the text
Large print edition designed by
Bernadette Montalvo.
Composed in 18 pt Plantin
on a Xyvision 300/Linotron 202N
by Stephen Traiger
of G.K. Hall & Co.